I0574506

THE HUNT FOR RAUBGOLD

WHERE THE PAST MEETS THE PRESENT

KATHERINE BURLAKE

Edited by: Marilyn Silverman
Book Consultant: Judith Briles, The Book Shepherd
Cover Design: Nathan Dasco
Interior and eBook conversion: Bublish

ISBN: 978-1-647046-30-9 (eBook)
ISBN: 978-1-647046-31-6 (paperback)

Denmark
Sylt Island
Husum
Baltic Sea
North Sea
Neustrelitz
Wismar
Ravensbruck
Hamberg
Hohenlychen
Berlin
Germany
Leipzig
Weimar
Cologne
Merkers
Frankfurt
Nuremburg
Munich
Vienna
Lake Toplitz
Austria
Zurich
Bern
Switzerland
Geneva

Cast of Characters

Ace Alfred Prowers; Amy's cousin; Sonora's nephew

Bazyli Czartoryski Russian neo-Nazi leader living outside Vienna, Austria

Bob Morris Friend of Prowers family; former CIA station chief, now retired

Count Lliessle Sonora's husband; heir to a banking fortune, deceased

Frederic Thoren's brother; banker, transported gold to Switzerland

Klaus Meyer Owner of Theodor Storm Hotel in Husum; German security service agent

Luca Manages Lliessle Bank in Zurich

Marton Works for Berlin Museum, translates old German; double agent

Misha Monk in Vilnius; the Abbot's brother

Sig Right-hand man of Bazyli Czartoryski, outside Vienna

Simon Bell German government security official

Sonora Prowers Lliessle Amy's and Ace's aunt

The Abbot Head of St. Benedict's Monastery, outskirts of Berlin

Thoren Employee of Sonora Lliessle; Frederic's brother

Vince Amy's first husband; searched for gold, deceased

Places and Organizations of Interest

AfD *Alternative für Deutschland*, far right-wing party in Germany.

BfV *Bundesamt für Verfassungsschutz*, or Federal Office for the Protection of the Constitution.

Berlin Capital of Germany. After being bombed to the ground in World War II, it is once again the city to visit in Europe. Museums, galleries, food, and clothing all make the city the trendiest of places.

Blénder "Kaleidoscope" in old German; "what you see is always changing."

Bullion vaults Private and government bullion storage vaults in the Swiss Alps.

The Committee Sonora Lliessle and selected world leaders.

Documentation Center Nazi Party Rallying Grounds; Museum in Nuremberg where former Nazi Party rallies were held. The permanent exhibition *Fascination and Terror* shows the causes, connections, and consequences of Nazi Germany.

Grey Eagles Right-wing, neo-Nazi political club run by the Czartoryskis.

Husum Small city in northern Germany with colorful houses and an inner harbor.

Lake Toplitz Lake in the mountain forest in the Austrian Alps; many believe the Nazis hid their gold in the lake, though none has yet been found.

Leipzig Located south of Berlin; once the center of Europe.

Neo-Nazis Post–World War II militant, social, and political movement; aim is to reinstate Nazi ideology.

Neustrelitz Located on the Zierker See in Müritz National Park, eighty minutes north of Berlin.

Raubgold Term used for the gold stolen by the Nazis in World War II.

Vatican Bank Established in 1942, the function of the bank is to provide safekeeping and administration of property for religious and charity works.

Vilnius Capital of Lithuania, the second-largest country in the Baltics.

Zurich Largest city in Switzerland, home to many financial institutions and banking companies.

Preface

Gold built the Third Reich's war machine and financed Nazis who escaped at the end of World War II with the dream of building the Fourth Reich. How much gold did the Nazis confiscate? How much has been found? No one knows. Today, in the twenty-first century, amateur and professional treasure seekers and neo-Nazis continue to search for *Raubgold*, the stolen Nazi gold.

CHAPTER ONE

The Search for the Stolen Gold Begins

ASUNCION, PARAGUAY, 2019

"We are broke. Marton, without the gold, our dream of a Fourth Reich is dead." The man with a gray-white beard, known as Old Fritz, looked at Marton, whom the party was counting on to find the gold.

He really is a blénder: *what you see is what you get.*

He hoped the young man was stronger than he looked. Raising his beer stein, he said, "I toast the New Nazi Party as it rises here in Paraguay. Drink up, my friend; you have a long flight to Germany."

Marton finished his beer and looked around the bar in the Blue Boar Restaurant. Located on the outskirts of Asuncion,

Paraguay, it was a popular meeting place for former Nazis and their families.

I am a German, and here, thousands of miles away, I am surrounded by a room full of young, physically fit men of German descent.

All the men were passionate believers in the new Nazi Party, though few had ever been out of Paraguay or South America. What they needed to finance the New Reich, often called the Fourth Reich, was the gold that was hidden by the Nazis during World War II.

In his pocket, Marton touched the letter he found after his father's death. He knew the contents by heart. The Nazis had a scheme to ship the gold out of Germany. Unfortunately, the war ended sooner than expected, leaving the gold stranded in Germany.

So much for German efficiency, he thought.

For now, he sipped his beer. Old Fritz was right. The flight back to Germany was a long one.

• • •

VAIL, COLORADO, UNITED STATES

The driving wind and snow had kept Amy Prowers awake most of the night. Now, she was startled by the sound of an explosion. Her mountain home shuddered, then there was silence. She opened her eyes and looked at the digital clock. Four in the morning.

She turned on the outside lights and opened the blinds, and she saw that the cascading snow had turned the resort into a winter wonderland, perfect for early winter skiing. A wall of snow and ice had careened down the mountains and smashing into the teak deck above the garage. Otherwise, the home, designed for such events in the mountains of Vail appeared to be intact.

Despite the early hour she put on a parka and went downstairs opening the door leading to the garage. The back of the garage had been blasted open. All she could do was try to shovel the snow out of the garage.

The shovel hit something that had been hidden behind the back wall. She scraped the snow off part of a tattered but still intact, leather bag.

Amy smiled and shook her head, unable to believe what she had uncovered. Despite the snowy mess, she was looking at a beaten-up old leather bag, Vince's bag. The bag was believed lost when Vince, her first husband, was killed. How ironic to find the bag twenty years after his death.

She opened it and saw papers wrapped in waterproof packaging—a journal and a map that Vince had used in his hunt for *Raubgold*, the stolen Nazi gold. Everyone thought the journal and the map were lost when he died.

Obviously, we were wrong.

She started to call her Aunt Sonora but thought, *why bother?* She was flying to Berlin to see her for an extended visit at the end of the week. She would surprise her aunt with the bag.

Out the window, there was no sign of the winter storm. The sun shining on the snow made it a picture-perfect Colorado skiing day. She looked at the bag. What secrets did the map and journal hold? After all these years, maybe now she would find out.

CHAPTER TWO

Vince's Search for the Nazi Gold

BERLIN, GERMANY

Amy watched her aunt pour their favorite German brandy into crystal glasses. Sonora, elegantly dressed in a red pantsuit, her hair tinted light gray, looked as if she was attending one of her Committee meetings. Despite her age, she was very thin, which accentuated her height. Amy was never sure how she managed to stay so thin. Sonora never exercised and was always eating and drinking. Amy reminded herself that she had promised her aunt she would attend all the Committee meetings this year, even though she was not particularly interested. She liked the business of running Prowers companies, not the politics that Sonora seemed to feed on. But a promise was a promise.

Standing next to the stone fireplace in the Lliessle's nineteenth-century Berlin mansion, she could hear the oak logs crackle as they warded off the chilly fall days. The house had survived World War II, and her aunt had spent decades renovating it. It had been perfect for Committee meetings—until they went online. Her cousin Ace loved the new technology, while Sonora hated it.

"I want to look into their eyes," she always said.

Today, Amy needed her aunt's help to interpret the meaning of the map and the journal's contents. But it could wait. Drinking brandy was a Prowers tradition.

And to think, she thought, *we are really just two girls from the Colorado and Texas prairies.*

Amy unzipped the leather bag.

"So, what's in the bag? A gift?" her aunt asked.

"Something from the past. Something we thought was dead and gone."

"Oh my God. Is that what I think it is?" said Sonora. "I thought that bag was lost when Vince died. With the Prowers seal on the side, I'd know it anywhere. How did you find it?"

"A gift from the avalanche. After it crushed the garage wall, a hidden space behind the wall where Vince hid the bag opened up. He kept every piece of junk he ever found, but hiding the bag was unusual—even for him. He never was sneaky."

"To think, twenty years ago," said Sonora, "we thought the bag was destroyed when terrorists blew up his truck in northern Pakistan. Why he went to such an extent to conceal it or keep it safe . . . I guess we'll never know." She paused and laughed. "I made it sound like something out of a spy novel."

Amy laughed. "Vince's life was a spy novel."

Vince never had a grave. She had scattered his ashes in the Karakorum Range, where he had died. With that, he was gone; now, he was back. Somehow, she was not surprised.

Sonora opened the map very carefully since it was so old. "I wonder if it holds the secret of where the Nazi gold might be hidden. I hope there's a place marked with an *X*."

Amy looked over Sonora's shoulder at the map. "Berlin is the only city I recognize. The map is just a bunch of rivers and towns, but it must show the location of the gold mentioned in the journal."

Sonora opened the journal, also very carefully, and flipped the pages. "The language in this journal is a mixture of archaic German and Old Latin. It's an odd combination, likely designed to make it difficult for the average man to understand. It will take a linguistic specialist to translate; fortunately, I know one at the Berlin Museum.

"Marton is the son of one of the Count's long-time employees. I see him from time to time at the museum, and he attends the parties I throw for museum staff. He worked with your father and with Vince and then with my husband before he died. Is it possible that it's been almost five years since the Count died? And Vincent's death . . . That was almost twenty years ago?"

Amy looked at the journal. "What I remember is that Vince always said he was looking for the lost Nazi gold. But he went to Pakistan following some lead on Alexander the Great's tomb, because everyone thinks the grave is in Egypt. Yet he made it clear to me his mission was to find the gold."

Why had Vince deliberately hidden the bag in the false wall? What other secrets had he kept before he left for Pakistan? He didn't plan to die, but then, who does?

"Amy, Vince spent the last month of his life here in Berlin."

"Yes," said Amy with regret, remembering she had been in Mexico negotiating oil leases. "I wasn't in Berlin. The price of oil had taken a dive, and I wanted a piece of the new wells in the Gulf of Mexico. The price of oil rarely stayed down, at least not in that decade, so you had to move fast to buy it cheap. In those days, I couldn't do it from Berlin. Do you remember what Vince and my father were doing in Berlin?"

Sonora adjusted her diamond bracelet and looked disgusted. "They were secretive, and I never asked why. Now, I think they may have been afraid of something or someone. Marton might remember more details. He helped them with the ancient translations. The three were very chummy."

Amy hoped Sonora was right about the German, Marton. When Vince and her father were alive, they had traipsed around the world searching for lost antiquities. She was content to stay in Colorado and run the family oil and gas businesses.

Sonora looked at Amy, then back to the journal and the map. "Vince, sometimes alone, sometimes with your father's help, spent months looking and got nowhere."

"Sonora, that's just the point. They had two or three quests going on. Like Alexander the Great's grave and the Amber Room, Russia's most priceless works of art looted by the Nazis." She stopped and took a deep breath. "As you know, I was never into those searches. Now, twenty years have passed since Vince's death. Through an accident of nature, I found his map and his journal. I think it's a sign that I should try and finish his search for the gold. I hope I am not being disrespectful, but of my three husbands, he was the first and my true love."

She paused. "I need to make it up to him even if twenty years have passed."

Sonora poured more brandy into their glasses. "Amy, you're fifty years old, and I'm just over sixty. Twenty years ago, when Vince was looking for the gold, so were others. But today, the search for gold is a worldwide phenomenon. Only God knows how many searches are going on today in Germany by every political splinter group."

Amy looked at her aunt. "I won't feel like a failure if I don't find the gold. But I have to try." She paused for a moment. "I honestly think it's out there. It's lost. By looking, I feel I can validate all the work Vince did. Does that make sense?"

Sonora smiled. "Yes, it does. And Amy, I'll do what I can to help you." She picked up the map and the journal. "So many groups and individuals looking for the gold. In today's market, if found, it has to be worth over a billion dollars."

Amy agreed. "Vince always said it wasn't the value in money but what it represents in lives. To him, it was the souls of those who died in World War II—civilians, military, the people in the camps. The gold would be a testimony to their lives. He didn't want them forgotten and I am sure he wanted their descendants to have a share of the gold. That's why I'm going to try and find it. Does that make sense?"

"Yes," said Sonora. She lifted her crystal glass in a toast to Amy.

Amy looked at the bag that contained Vince's last adventure. His death never brought her closure. She always felt that he was still out there searching. Now, after all these years, she would try to find out where the map and the journal would take her. Maybe she could bring closure for both of them.

When he was alive, she thought, *his search for gold was a search for fool's gold. Now, I have a real reason for the search. To think, all it took was a winter storm in Vail.*

"One of the last things Vince did before leaving for Pakistan was to go to Vilnius to meet a monk. Why the trip to the capital of Lithuania? Maybe the monk he met knows something."

Sonora agreed. "That monk's brother is the Abbot of St. Benedict's Monastery here in Berlin. I'll give him a call, see if his brother is still in Vilnius. If he is, maybe he can help you."

"Whether he's alive or not, I'm following Vince's footsteps. I'm going to Vilnius," Amy said. "I want to try and find out, after all these years, what Vince was doing." She had no idea what that might be. "Sonora, I don't know if I'll find the gold, but I must try, or I'll regret it. I owe Vince a search."

"I agree," said Sonora. "The last thing I want is for these right-wing political groups to find it. If they do, it will finance their activities into the next century. One of these groups is led by the Czartoryski family. Now, they live in Vienna, but before the war, they lived for centuries in Vilnius. I always wondered what Vince found so interesting in that city. If you meet the monk, you can ask him."

"Sonora, there must be something to the lost gold. So many people are looking for it."

Sonora laughed. "Gold drives men. Remember, most of the people who knew about the gold, or hid it, have died. When I think of this, I remind myself that the Germans are detail-oriented people, so somewhere, there must be a record since they keep duplicates, if not triplicates, of everything."

CHAPTER THREE

Was the Nazi Gold Ever Here?

VILNIUS, LITHUANIA

The sun was setting as the train pulled into the Vilnius railroad station. The receding light reflected on the stucco buildings, the carved roofs, and the narrow streets with flower boxes in every window. Amy found them a welcome change from the forests and rolling hills she'd traveled through hour after hour on the train from Berlin.

The train jerked to a halt. She picked up her small bag and stepped out on the platform. First, she would find a hotel and ask the manager to see if he could get her a flight back to Berlin. The train seemed to take forever.

She spoke to the conductor, saying the words *taxi* and *hotel*, thankful those words were the same in any language. The conductor pointed to her right.

"Hotel Panama," he answered in perfect English.

Amy had forgotten how many people in Eastern Europe spoke English as well as she did. She knew the word *hotel* was the same in any language. When she asked the cab driver for the Hotel Panama, he answered in perfect English that the hotel was across the square.

At the hotel, Amy heard a din of voices coming from a bar on the other side of the lobby.

"Bar best in city. We have our own brewery," said Jonas, who had to be the tallest hotel manager in Vilnius. "First beer on me."

"Vilnius beer, I have been told, is some of the best in the world," said Amy as she checked in.

"*Ja*, is best. It is because of . . . how you say in America . . . our microbreweries."

Amy looked through the open doorway and could see people eating.

"I have a favor to ask. Is it possible for me to get a flight back to Berlin—maybe tomorrow afternoon or evening?"

Jonas told her that would be no problem. He motioned to a bellman, whom Amy followed up the sweeping wooden staircase, glad the rooms were only one floor up. As they arrived on the darkened floor, the lights slowly came on.

"In the days when the Communists ran our country, they would turn the lights on when the tourists checked in. Saved electricity," said the bellman. "The Communists are gone, but the practice remains."

When she opened the door, she saw a simple room, clean and warm.

What more can I want? she thought.

She pulled off her boots, put on a pair of leather loafers, and headed down the stairs to the bar.

Waving hello to Jonas, Amy hoped the bar would be full of local people, not tourists. She wasn't disappointed; they were definitely locals. Everyone's hair was some shade of blond, which had to come from their Nordic heritage. No designer clothes—just jeans and sweaters. They were all tall like Jonas. Amy knew she could pass for a local with her light-brown hair, gray eyes, and fair complexion. And she was tall.

The beer arrived, cold and delicious. She picked up the menu, which was written in German and Russian and featured pictures.

She pointed to fish and chips and said, "Beer," holding her hands apart to indicate she wanted a large beer. *Beer* was another word that was the same in any language.

The food arrived, and with it, a monk, who slipped into a chair at her table. His robe was gray, matching his short, gray beard. She could see from the lines on his face that he was very old.

He spoke in almost perfect English. "I am Misha. My brother is the Abbot of St. Benedict's Monastery in Berlin. Your aunt called my brother and asked him if I would help you. Both the Count and Sonora have been supporters of the monastery, even during the years when the Berlin Wall was up. That was tricky because the monastery was on the east side of the wall. But your aunt and her husband managed it."

The man's eyes were bright as his wrinkled hands tightened around the glass of beer he had brought to the table. "By way of introduction, I was the assistant to the director at the Museum of History and Ethnography here in Vilnius. I am Polish, German, and a Benedictine monk. In Vilnius, we have over ninety nationalities. Before the Great War, our city was called the Jerusalem of Europe. I spent my life with more Russians, Poles, and Jews than Lithuanians." He paused. "Someone told me that more Lithuanians live in America than Vilnius."

Amy said it sounded reasonable and ordered more beer, including another one for the monk. She had almost finished her meal and was starting to feel like herself. She was no longer queasy from the motion of the train. There was no point in wasting time.

"You know I'm looking for the gold my husband tried to find so many years ago."

He nodded. "The Nazi gold. I remember your husband, Vincent, right, and his search. He was the first person I ever heard call it *Raubgold*, the word for stolen Nazi gold. Tomorrow, I come early with a driver. I show you where gold was first hidden on the Czartoryski Estate that was bombed at the end of World War II. That was the gold your husband was trying to find before he died."

"How do you know so much about the gold?" asked Amy.

Brother Misha said all wars end in chaos on the ground and in the air. "Miss Prowers, you must realize nobody was in charge. Russian troops were running through the city, going east and west. I was at the Czartoryski home outside Vilnius.

They had lived there since the fourteenth or fifteenth century, but during World War II, the old prince left another home near Krakow in southern Poland. Today, the family lives in Vienna. Before he left Vilnius, the prince told me he was giving several paintings as a gift to our monastery outside Berlin. My younger brother, who was not yet the Abbot, was anxious to receive them.

"With several monks, we went to pick up the paintings. To our surprise, two Russian military trucks were unloading wooden boxes, storing them in the Czartoryski home. We never saw what was in them, but the old caretaker told us in confidence the boxes held gold. Gold the Germans had stolen—or maybe the Russians."

"How fortunate for you," said Amy, which was not what she was thinking, but if she wanted to keep him talking, she had to say something. "Why would the Russians store gold in Vilnius?"

He sipped his beer. "Everyone knew the Americans and British were going to attack anything that moved on the roads. They had to store it until things cleared up." He threw up his hands, miming an explosion, and took another drink.

"So, the gold was in the Czartoryski house?" asked Amy.

"*Da, da*, but nothing is perfect in war." He looked at her with a smile. "Sounds simple, *da*? But it was not. After the war, the troubles began."

Misha looked around the noisy bar, as if someone was listening, and lowered his voice. Amy had to lean forward to hear him. She wondered if someone was watching them.

"Stalin knew about the gold. He sent a personal emissary to follow up on what everyone said were stories, but everyone believed them to be true. The Russian from Moscow spent time in Vilnius. You heard, I am sure, stories about Stalin, *da*?"

"Yes."

"The emissary told Stalin the gold got as far as Vilnius, where any trace of it disappeared. Stalin believed this story because the gold never surfaced again. When Stalin died, the search stopped for the Russians but not for the locals. About five years ago, a German named Frederic was often in and out of the Czartoryski compound. Everyone knew he was a big-time stock investor. Some thought he was going to invest in Vilnius's businesses. They were wrong. He was after the gold."

Misha paused and looked directly at Amy. "Frederic knew the Lliessle family from his investment work with the Lliessle Bank. He got his brother Thoren a job in Sonora's household."

More drinks arrived, and Amy asked Misha if he had ever met Stalin. He hadn't, but he had heard stories about Stalin. Amy wasn't interested in Stalin but listened, wondering why she made this trip to Vilnius. The information could have been conveyed on the phone.

Well, she thought, *I'm here, and I should see the Czartoryski house.*

Misha looked around again. Amy wondered if someone was following him but thought it impolite to ask. Afterall, she just met him. He spoke quietly.

"The Nazis and Hitler did not like Vilnius. Not because it was Polish but because they thought of it as Jewish. They missed what made the city important. We are close to the Baltic Sea and to the port of Klaipeda. It is the largest ice-free port on the Baltic and has huge shipyards. From that port, the Nazis planned to take their gold to South America. I told Vince all of this.

"Everyone has heard about the gold found in a mine in southern Germany; it was worth a few hundred million dollars. I tell you, the Nazis had a couple of billion. They looted the national banks of every country they conquered. The gold was figured in tons of bullion because the price changes. It is still out there and worth even more today. Miss Prowers, what I tell you is true."

"On that note, let's have one more drink," said Amy. "Can your driver pick me up at nine in the morning? If we have an early start, I can get a flight back to Berlin in the afternoon."

"Will have a driver pick you up at hotel. I go with you."

He made it sound easy, but Amy intuitively felt something still wasn't right about what they were doing. She wasn't sure what to do except to see the Czartoryski house and return to Berlin. She knew Sonora was trying to get a translation of the ancient journal she had found with the map. Maybe it would tell them where the gold was, though that was being awfully optimistic. It couldn't be that easy, or Vince would have found the gold.

Amy had finished her drink, but the monk was still sipping his. She thought he was delaying. Then, he spoke. "Miss Prowers, it is important that you know this. Gold is a commodity that buys something. We all know that. This gold, this *Raubgold*, has another meaning. It represents the souls of those who were killed in World War II. Not just the concentration camp victims but also the civilians and military in so many countries in Europe. Do you understand, Miss Prowers?"

"Now, I do. Vince said the gold represented people. Does that mean if we find the gold, we find their souls?"

Misha laughed. "No, but when it is found, it will not be a commodity but will represent their lives, and that will determine how it will be spent."

"I'll drink to that," said Amy.

They clinked their glasses in a toast.

• • •

In the morning, Misha was late leaving the monastery, which was located behind the cathedral. He was late because the gardener stopped him with questions about what to plant in the garden. Any other time, he would have enjoyed the conversation—but not today. It was more important that he meet Amy.

As he rushed out the side gate of the monastery, he didn't notice the person standing on the street, which was odd, since the night before, in the restaurant, he kept looking around, thinking someone was watching him. By the time he realized what was happening, it was too late.

Someone grabbed him from behind, and he felt the sudden pain of a knife thrust into his back. He wasn't dead when he hit the pavement, but he may as well have been. Murders were common in Vilnius. His death was now just another statistic.

I am an old man, he thought as the blood rushed out of his body. His last thought was that at least he had told Amy about the gold.

• • •

The morning was clear but chilly; after all, it was fall, and winter was on its way. Amy drank a cup of coffee and waited for Misha and the driver. Neither showed up. Frustrated, she asked Jonas, the hotel manager, for help. He said the Czartoryski house was easy to find. Even better, the taxi driver he called spoke English.

Fifteen minutes later, the taxi pulled up beside a broken iron gate and turned down a dirt road into a forest. After a few hundred yards, she saw the overgrown ruins.

"This is the edge of town?" asked Amy.

"*Ja.*"

The driver stayed in the cab while Amy walked around the ruins. All that remained of the house were crumbling stucco walls barely taller than her head. She returned to the taxi, wondering why the family had never rebuilt the home. She asked the driver, "If they were nobility, did they lose their fortune in the war?"

"Oh, no," said the driver, who turned out to be a wealth of information about the Czartoryskis. "They are still very rich and live in Vienna. They own a bank in Vilnius, a hotel in Paris, and have money from America—reparations for the war. I think they have an agricultural plant in southern Poland. Some of the local people believe they have a hoard of Nazi gold. Who can say?"

Amy had no idea who the Czartoryskis were but was eager to get back to Berlin. She hoped Jonas had gotten her a late afternoon flight.

As the taxi pulled away, she looked back at the ruins. There was an eerie aura about the place. Was someone watching her?

She saw no one but realized she was acting like Misha, looking over her shoulder for some phantom bad guy.

• • •

When Amy arrived at the hotel, she saw the staff clustered around Jonas. He was visibly upset.

"Bad news, Miss Prowers. The old monk is dead. It is the monk you met last night in the bar."

Amy asked what happened, thinking that since he was an old man, he had a heart attack.

"He was found in front of the monastery with a knife in his back. Murdered. Our country for years has had the highest murder rate in Europe. Still, I do not see why the old monk would be killed."

Amy expressed regrets but wasn't sure what else to say or what she could do. The monk's murder upset her. Did their meeting yesterday have anything to do with his death? She didn't know, but now, she had to get back to Berlin.

"I didn't know the monk, and I have no reason to stay." She looked at Jonas. "You have my address and my phone number in Berlin. If the authorities need me, they'll know where to find me."

"I understand. Made a plane reservation for you to Berlin, as you asked," said Jonas.

"Thank you," said Amy, relieved to be spared the long train trip. But Jonas had more to say.

"My personal driver will take you to the airport. I want to be sure you get there." He hesitated for a moment. "Miss Prowers, I do not want you to worry, but after you left yesterday in the taxi, a man asked about you and the monk. He was an odd fellow. He spoke German, but I am not sure he was a German. Knew his way around Vilnius. You know anyone here?"

Amy shook her head. Someone knew she was here and meeting the monk. But who? Neither she nor her aunt thought the connection with the monk would be dangerous. Should she have been killed, not the monk?

An hour later, at the airport bar, waiting for the flight, she ordered a vodka. Had the trip been a waste of time? What about the innuendos about the Czartoryski family? Brother Misha, her contact, was killed, and the so-called guy who spoke German was looking for her. The one thing she knew for sure was that searching for the gold was not going to be easy.

She finished her vodka as the loudspeaker announced her flight to Berlin. As she went through the gate, her mind was on Vince. The search for the gold was important to him. He always said the gold represented the souls of the millions of people killed in World War II. When he died, both she and her Aunt Sonora believed his searches were over.

Now, she thought, *it was unbelievable that the search has started again.*

CHAPTER FOUR

Back in Berlin

"Ace is flying in tomorrow," said Sonora. "He called from Dubai and said he was tired of listening to empty words from the oil potentates at the conference. The Middle East Oil Conference is running for two more days, but Ace said he's heard enough. Today, the world has a glut of oil, so he thinks finding the map and the journal in Vail is more important than the Prowers oil business."

Amy laughed. She and Ace inherited the Prowers oil and gas business, but she knew the meeting in Dubai must have bored him stiff.

Sonora spread the ancient map on the table. She told Amy this was a copy, as she had stored the original map and journal in a safe-deposit box at the bank.

Looking at the map, Amy said, "Sonora, we're back to square one. All I recognize is Berlin."

"I'm with you. Berlin is all I recognize," Sonora said. "Ace is an expert on reading maps, so hopefully, he can figure it out. I got him a room at the Kempinski, since you're staying in the apartment. That apartment comes in handy, because the hotel always gets us another room when we need it. Like you, Ace loves the location. Says it's centrally located to the restaurants and clubs."

She looked at her niece. "Amy, our problem is finding someone who can translate the journal. As I said before, it's in ancient German. Marton worked with Vince. I have an investigator who checks out the background of anyone who works with our family. His father worked with the Count in Switzerland during World War II. I know Marton from his work at the Berlin Museum. I like him, but the background check shows he's a neo-Nazi.

"Today in Germany, they're called right-wingers. If I understand my investigator, Marton is a leader in the movement, not just in Germany but around the world. How he got involved, no one is sure. The investigator is still looking into his background, but regardless of Marton's politics, I believe he can help us with the translations. I'll give him a call." She paused. "Political affiliations are in flux today in Germany."

Amy felt as if she was traveling in circles. "The trip to Vilnius was worthless. Misha, the elderly monk, was killed. I talked to him the day before his death and he seemed worried, almost like he had a premonition. He remembered that Vince was looking for the Nazi gold. *Raubgold* was what he called it."

Sonora agreed that the monk being killed right after talking to her was suspicious, but neither of them could say why. Was it just a coincidence, or was it something sinister?

"I don't think we can read too much into it," said Sonora. "For years, Vilnius had the number one murder rate in all the European Union countries. The monk could be another statistic, but we can't be sure. I'm more concerned about the German who seemed interested in you and the monk."

Amy looked at Sonora. "So, where do we go from here?"

Sonora smiled. "Nowhere, except stay alert. Certain right-wing groups in this country would do almost anything to find that gold. We have to be careful."

She went on to say one of the largest right-wing groups was the AfD, Alternative for Germany, now the third-largest political party in Germany. "Some think they're just right-wingers—or nutters, just crazy people—but to me, they're dangerous. And Amy, as you look for the gold, watch out for them. They look like other Germans but aren't like them."

"Understood," said Amy.

"Good," said Sonora. "Despite what you think, your trip was useful. The monk, Misha, confirmed what Vince was searching for the gold. I wish the monk was still alive, but his brother, real brother, is the Abbot of St. Benedict's Monastery on the east side of Berlin. I called him to express regrets at his brother's death. You need to do the same.

"To be honest, I wonder what the Abbot really knows. He was in the monastery during the years when it was behind the wall in East Germany and was controlled by the Russians. He has had a front-row seat to all of the changes in this city."

"So, what's next?" asked Amy.

"Ace follows the activities of the new Nazi groups, who can't be called Nazis here in Germany. He sees them as a problem for the government of Germany, but his information has been useful for the Committee. Coincidences happen. Like Vince's plane crashing near the site of a 1947 plane crash in the woods in central England. Everyone in the 1947 crash died, including the two passengers who were officials with the Bank of England. Vince landed on their crash site in his parachute."

Amy interrupted her. "I never understood—even then, and I was there—why those bank officials were important. I mean, the bag with the journal and the map could have been buried in the woods by anyone."

"True," said Sonora, "but more likely, it was on the plane with the bank officials and was thrown into the woods when the plane crashed. During World War II, allegations were made that the Bank of England held Nazi gold in accounts in other banks in Europe, particularly in Switzerland. Each of the fourteen countries the Nazis invaded had a national bank with gold bullion, which was confiscated by the Third Reich. The banks also had gold coins. Adding to that gold, the Nazis confiscated gold from Jews and from political prisoners and melted their gold into bars. A bank in Switzerland engraved the bars as if they had been stored in the Berlin Reichsbank for years."

Now, Amy understood. "So, the Lliessle Bank, like the Bank of England, was able to move gold from Switzerland around Europe, or to South America, where former Nazis went to hide."

Sonora smiled. "Doesn't matter where the right-wingers live. South America or Germany, they're still Nazis. These right-wingers believe in the tenets of Nazism. That means they're ultranationalist, racist, and homophobic. Most of all, they're anti-Semitic. They want to institute the Fourth Reich, deny the Holocaust, and glorify Hitler. A real nice bunch of people who never let facts stand in the way of reality."

In Germany, Amy knew, neo-Nazi activities were banned. She also knew that money was needed to keep the movement going.

"The stolen gold taken out of Germany after World War II," Sonora said, "funded their operations and their lifestyles. Over the decades, that gold has been spent; the money's gone. Today, they need the rest of the gold that never left Germany.

"That's why this map in the rotting leather bag Vince found is important. It most likely shows where the gold is hidden. All we have to do is figure out that hiding spot. The map has Berlin as the center point in northern Germany. Most of the other searches by right-wingers and by treasure hunters focus on southern Germany and Austria. We may be the only ones looking in northern Germany. To me, it makes sense to take the gold out by U-boat. Why bury the gold in the south of Germany, miles away from any seaport?"

Sonora went on to say that the Allies, in 1945, found about two hundred eighty million dollars in gold bars in the Merkers mine in southern Germany.

"Everyone knows about the find in the Merkers mine. A number of books have been written about the find, and a movie, *The Monuments Men*, was made about it. Since the end of the war, political groups, both right and left wing, have been looking for the rest of the gold but have come up empty-handed. Most gold hunters believe that several billion dollars in bullion is still lying in the ground in Germany or Switzerland, waiting to be found."

"Brother Misha wasn't specific," said Amy, "but he told me that the gold, during World War II, was to be shipped out of ports in the north. That might have been his way of telling me to look north. He also reminded me that Vince said that the gold represented people. It's not a commodity to be traded."

Sonora said she remembered Amy's father and Vince talking about what the gold represented. "I wanted to ask them—but never did—how the gold could bring back the millions of people that had died. Maybe it's best, Amy, to leave the dead buried. I think we need outside help. Bob Morris sent me an email. He's retiring from the CIA and is in Switzerland. I'll give him a call."

Remembering Bob from Saudi Arabia, Amy was relieved to have an expert like Bob help them. He had run one of the biggest intelligence units in the Middle East. If he was in Europe, then he must have contacts and a reason to be here, retired or not. And she knew her aunt would make it worth his while.

"He'll be a big help."

Sonora reached for a bottle of brandy and poured two glasses. They both knew they would do everything to find out where the map would lead them.

CHAPTER FIVE

St. Benedict's Monastery

St. Benedict's Monastery had been a fixture on the southeast side of Berlin for over a thousand years. During the Russian occupation, the main hall of the monastery was used as a convention center. In the 1990s, it was converted back to a monastery.

Today, the Abbot enjoyed the solitude of watching the rhythmic flow of the Spree River. His job wasn't stressful, but today, that had changed. The postmark on Misha's letter indicated it was sent from Vilnius. He noticed the letter was sent the day before his brother was killed.

Though the Abbot was twenty years younger than Misha, he recalled how Misha used to follow him around on their grandfather's estate outside Dresden. In those days of riding horses and fishing, neither of them would have thought this was how it would end.

And my own end is yet to come, he thought.

He scanned the letter again, reading what his brother had written:

> *My brother, the past has returned. Remember years ago, maybe two decades, when the American, Vince, was convinced he knew where the gold was. He told me he had found a leather pouch with the seal of the Bank of England. Inside was a journal and a map. From what he could translate, the journal was in an old Germanic language. This American believed the treasure was still in Germany.*
>
> *Vince understood enough German to know there was more gold to be found, gold bullion taken from the national banks of the countries the Nazis had conquered. He believed the map showed the location.*
>
> *For an American, he was very careful, and he would never show me either the journal or the map.*
>
> *God intervened. Vince traveled to Pakistan, of all the Godforsaken places, and never returned. We forgot about him. But we never forgot about the gold.*
>
> *Now, his spirit is back, reincarnated, in his wife, Amy Prowers. She told me she found her*

long-dead husband's journal in their mountain home. She did not mention the map, but I believe she found it, so why not tell me? I don't know. And it is very likely that she didn't know Vince told me about the map.

I wanted to tell her the truth about the gold but was distracted. I thought I saw Marton in the café across from the Panama Hotel. But I wasn't sure.

I do not know what else to say. I am sending you this because you must know we are both in danger. Marton will stop at nothing to find the gold. He belongs to the Grey Eagles.

The gold taken after the war is gone. More money is needed to fund right-wing activities. Though some of the right-wingers have jobs, many do not even work, just attend right-wing protests.

Stay well, my brother, but keep your eyes open.

It was signed "Misha."

He put the letter down. Misha was killed the day after it arrived. A random street mugging, according to the Vilnius police. The police missed the point. The hit on Misha was not random—of that, the Abbot was sure.

The new-age Nazi groups were running out of money. Many had gotten jobs to support themselves and their families. That reduced the time they had to promote their cause and establish the Fourth Reich. Scattered around the world, they exhausted funds smuggled out of Germany before the end of World War II. Now, they needed the rest of the gold bullion in Germany.

What would the dollar value be today? The Abbot thought for a moment—a billion, two billion. No way to be sure since no one was certain how much had been stolen during World War II.

Not all Nazis were convinced the war would end with a victory, especially after the failure to capture Stalingrad in 1943. It was then that the SS and army officers moved money out of Germany and into Swiss bank accounts. The Swiss banks transferred their money to South America. How much was sent to South America . . . no one seemed to know.

Marton's father, working for Count Lliessle in Switzerland, assisted the Nazis in making bank transfers of illegal funds look legitimate. Unfortunately for the Nazis, the war ended rapidly, leaving most of the gold in Germany.

He looked out again at the peaceful Spree River. How ironic that the American, Vince, accidently found a pouch from the Bank of England with a journal and the map. Vince had been an idealist and an amateur. He dabbled in archeology with his father-in-law and flew off to Pakistan like a fool, looking for Alexander the Great's grave.

None of that mattered now. He had to find a way to get the journal and the map. Both were necessary. The map to identify where where the Nazis' gold bullion was hidden, and the journal to interpret the map. He knew it was his destiny to find the gold. St. Benedict's Monastery in Berlin was generously funded from donations from the Lliessle Bank.

Sonora will help find the gold, he thought.

The Abbot knew Sonora didn't openly sponsor right-wing, neo-Nazi groups. At least, that was her public persona. She did run the Committee. Who knew, except the members, what their philosophy was?

Being one of the leaders in the Grey Eagles, a little-known but dominant neo-Nazi group whose goal was the formation of the Fourth Reich, the Abbot knew that finding the gold was a must. His membership with the group must remain confidential. Not even his brother Misha knew he had joined.

Amy Prowers had the journal and the map. He needed to talk to her, but he had to be careful since he wasn't sure of Amy's or Sonora's relationship to Marton, nor was he sure Marton's loyalties really were with the Grey Eagles. There was a word to describe Marton—the *blénder*. In German, it meant "what you see is not what you get." That was Marton. He was a kaleido-scope of faces, never allowing one to see the whole person. He hoped Marton was a Grey Eagle, but with a *blénder*, one could never be sure.

Looking out on the flowing water of the Oder-Spree Canal, the Abbot hoped his plan would flow as smoothly as the water of the canal. He had to meet Amy.

Should I call her or wait for Sonora to set up a meeting? he wondered.

CHAPTER SIX

Meeting Marton

In Leipzig, Marton crossed the square and headed down a small side street to a rathskeller tucked between two small clothing stores. The places Simon Bell picked to meet were a challenge. A senior agent with the Bundesamt für Verfassungsschutz, or BfV—the Federal Office for the Protection of the Constitution— Simon always believed someone was watching him. Marton knew his job was to ensure that no one was following him.

Marton looked like a spook was supposed to look: so unremarkable that he was totally invisible. No one would ever remember just what he looked like. Above average height, not overweight; only with his red-brown hair parted to the side did he resemble his father.

He had changed buses three times and now was in a local bar in a neighborhood that was anything but upscale. Marton couldn't get the idea out of his head that this meeting was like going to a funeral. Why he felt that way, he didn't know. He wasn't a spy like Simon Bell, but he felt like one.

Simon was supposed to be wearing a blue jacket.

Why, Marton wondered, *is the color of a coat being used for identification?*

Then, he saw the blue jacket in a booth near the back exit. Marton saw a wrinkled and lined face and a balding hairline. He thought Simon looked old, until he saw his eyes—a riveting blue, like his jacket—looking at him. He sat down as Simon ordered two beers.

Simon thanked him for making the trek to Leipzig, saying he wanted to be sure no one saw them together. Then, he got straight to the point. "I want you to tell me what you know about Amy Prowers's trip to Vilnius, what you did there, and what Sonora might know. I'm glad you followed Amy."

"Learned very little," said Marton.

Simon sipped his beer, then spoke softly. "You are our contact inside the Lliessle group. I am convinced you will learn from them where the gold is located. Intelligence tells us Amy is obsessive about finding the gold to fulfill her dead husband's dream. I need you to follow the family so we do not miss a move. An elderly monk, the Abbot's brother, was killed in Vilnius. I know Sonora will play down the death with the usual comments about Vilnius's high crime rate."

Marton looked directly into Simon's eyes, knowing he had to tell him. If Simon found out later, then he would be furious.

"I had no other way to shut the monk up except to put a knife in his back."

Simon paused and ordered more beer. "Marton, you should try the sausage—the best in central Germany. Though you know many think Regensburg or Nuremberg sausage is better."

Marton ordered a small platter, figuring Simon should know. He locked away the information that his contact very likely was from central Germany—or simply knew the area very well.

"Marton, that monk had been a problem for many years. Our organization several times discussed eliminating him. He had been around since the war and knew where the bodies were buried. For some reason, he started shooting his mouth off without thinking about what he was saying. Eliminating the monk was the right thing to do. No one will miss him. He might have made statements to incite the many crazy groups searching for the gold to focus on northern Germany. We have to watch the Abbot. Blood may be thicker than water. Will he avenge his brother's death?"

Despite Simon's comments, Marton's instincts told him the monk's death had been a mistake. "I can try to get information on what the Lliessle family may know. Sonora wants me to write a memoir about what her husband did during the war. She knows I worked with Vince on translating the journal, which may be what she wants today. Once I am considered part of her organization, I should be able to find out what the family is doing."

Simon agreed. "Keep your ear to the ground. You may hear something. I will send you a text if our contacts come up with something specific. You are the number one expert who can translate that ancient dialect in the journal. They need you. Beats me why the bank officials used that archaic language. They must have thought it was a code."

Marton grinned. "You have to admit that the dialogue keeps anyone from causally reading the journal. Please tell me we have other clues, other sources to find where the gold is hidden."

The old man looked tired. "I wish we did, and we should, but we do not."

According to Simon, the end of World War II came suddenly. The Nazi Party couldn't decide between storing the bullion in the mines in southern Germany or storing it in northern Germany, where it could be moved out by ship. One of the idiosyncrasies of the war was that the U-boats were targeted, but the Allies let cargo ships from neutral countries pass without incident.

"Back then, Nazi leadership was convinced that the northern ports were the way to ship gold to South America. Some gold had been sent to South America from Switzerland via Spain and Portugal. But in the past decades, it has been spent."

He looked at Marton as if he could see right through him.

"The gold is critical. Without it, the Fourth Reich ends before it begins. We need to find it before the right-wingers do."

Marton nodded that he understood.

Simon looked worried, causing Marton to ask, "So, the gold went north?"

"We think so. Part of our group, within the German government, has always believed that the gold went north and never left

Germany." Simon went on to say that in World War II, after the Reichsbank had sent its gold to Switzerland, more gold appeared. This gold was taken from the jewelry of prisoners in the camps. The Nazis built a refinery across the Oder River in Poland. If discovered, then they could blame the Poles and the Russians for stealing gold from prisoners.

"I am confident," said Simon, "that the old lady likes you, but Amy and Ace are the problem. You must convince them to take you on their search." He looked at Marton and grinned. "Focus on the gold. Do not get hung up on if Hitler was or was not killed in the bunker. Anytime gold is discussed, up comes the subject of Hitler's death. If he left Germany, naturally, he could not take the gold with him. Would be too obvious. Do you really think he died in the bunker? Doesn't matter. Today, he is dead."

Marton shrugged. "No, I do not think he died in the bunker. But it is decades-old history. When will we meet again?"

Simon laughed. "We will keep an eye on you and will find you."

As they said goodbye, Simon thrust two Nuremberg sausages into his bag for the train ride back to Berlin, saying these are the best.

As he got ready to leave, Marton wanted to ask Simon why he didn't tell him that Hitler had escaped and lived in South America. Then, he realized why. It didn't matter. That was past. Today, finding the stolen gold was what was important. The rest of the story was only about a ghost.

• • •

The train track ran alongside the Elbe River and through culti-vated fields in the German countryside. Small river ferries car-rying one or two cars took passengers from the east side to the west and back again.

Marton didn't notice the scenery. The trip on the train from Leipzig to Berlin took a little over two hours, but to him, it seemed like minutes. He kept going over in his mind how he could show Sonora he was able to research the Count's work. He didn't see how until he recalled the archives in Nuremberg, the so-called Documentation Center Museum.

As a museum curator, he had access to more files than the public. A trip to Nuremberg was next on his agenda. It was time for the Christmas markets. Good food and good drink. The files at the center might have information on Count Lliessle and what he might have done with the gold.

He needed a list of names of those who were known to be handling the gold. Old Fritz from Asuncion would know. He took out his phone to text him, thankful the old man was up-to-date on technology.

CHAPTER SEVEN

The Map and the Journal

Amy found herself in the library at Sonora's house, looking at the copy of the map. Because of her work with the Committee, Sonora had a range of maps and books from all over the world. Amy admired the many antiques. Her favorite was a small wooden chest with gold inlays that the Count had brought back from Yemen.

She turned back to the map. Ace was due to arrive today, provided there weren't any more delays for security reasons. She trusted Ace and knew he was an expert at reading maps. They had always been close, yet she was still surprised to find the odd areas where her cousin, the ex–Special Forces guy, was an expert. She didn't want to second-guess him, remembering all the years when Vince was obsessed with the map and with the journal. No one questioned him.

Taking a sip of wine, she recalled how Vince was always chasing some treasure in a remote part of the world. What was worse was that sometimes, her father was right there with him. Nothing was more important to Vince than the chase. He died hunting for Alexander the Great's tomb, but he should have died years before in the woods, when his Harrier jet flamed out, and he parachuted into an English woodland.

She remembered how he insisted on going back to the woods.

And I went with him.

Then, he spent hours researching how to interpret the journal and map that he found in the leather bag.

I didn't see what was so interesting, but Vince was convinced finding the bag was fate.

At a library in Cambridge, England, he found an article on a plane crash in the late 1960s, in the same little wooded forest, more than twenty years before his crash. That crash killed the pilot and two passengers, who were bank officials with the Bank of England.

He became obsessed with the two crashes. He couldn't get past the fact that the newspaper clippings said bank officials on the flight were believed to carry details on where the Nazi gold had been hidden. He was sure those officials were carrying the journal and the map. Vince concluded that the Nazi gold was worth billions. Where he got that figure, he could never say. Gold is measured in tons of bullion, so the value varies with the price.

She recalled how he had tried to find out more about the two passengers, the bank officials who had died in the crash. What he thought was unusual was that the London bank's branch in Switzerland had been mentioned in every publication discussing where the Nazis may have hidden their gold. Some coincidence, Vince called it. Amy wasn't so sure. Even back then, she thought anyone could have hidden the bag in the woods. Maybe she was just being cynical.

Though they all had some degree of expertise in German, the language in the journal was complex. Her father, when he was shown the journal, had been adamant that someone with linguistic skills was needed to accurately interpret the journal. He said the German language used was a thousand years old.

Linguistic skills, thought Amy.

Marton was the only person she and Sonora knew who could interpret it today. And he had helped Vince years ago. Vince let Marton's father read the diary. Then, the old man had died suddenly in an odd hiking accident in Switzerland. Even Sonora's husband, the Count, said the accident seemed suspicious.

The police believed the old man had a heart attack and refused to pursue the matter further. No one could tell the police that the man's primary job for the Count had been managing gold assets in the Count's private accounts as well as the family's bank in Switzerland.

Amy told herself to forget about what had happened more than twenty years ago and concentrate on what to do today. Moving a bar of gold, let alone multiple bars, was not a solitary activity. How could it have been done?

Looking out the window at the light drizzle, she picked up the phone to call Marton on the number Sonora had given her. He likely was a loyal neo-Nazi, as Sonora said, but he was the only expert they knew. Besides, Vince had trusted him to do translations so many years ago. Marton's phone went to voice mail, which said he was out of town and to leave a message.

Amy hung up, thinking the day was a loss until Ace arrived. She walked down the hallway to Sonora's office, where her aunt was sorting papers.

"In Berlin, a city of museums, is there a place I might research Nazi gold?"

Sonora thought for a moment. "Of course. I should have remembered Potsdam. Berlin was bombed to bits during the war. The Nazis knew that might happen and moved the records outside the city. A place to find information today would be Potsdam since the city was virtually untouched in the war. People think of it as the place where you can see the palace of Frederick the Great and the buildings where the Potsdam Conference took place after World War II. Today, it is full of pictures of Truman, Churchill, and Stalin.

"Southwest of Potsdam, in the suburb of Babelsberg, is a complex that services the film industry. The archives might have some information. This little suburb was the hub of German movies, though most had a propaganda theme. The library still exists. You might find something in the files."

Sonora said the library in Babelsberg was run independently from the museums and the libraries in Berlin.

"Do you think my German is good enough to translate?"

Her aunt was emphatic. "Yes. You can read German perfectly and understand conversations. Speaking is your weak suit. I would go with you, but I'm waiting for a call from a member of the Committee."

Sonora suggested that Amy should wait for Ace to arrive from Dubai, but Amy disagreed. "You're probably right, but I feel like I'd waste the day. If I find anything, Ace and I can always go back."

"I see you want to do something, so take Thoren. Then, you won't have to worry about driving or the language."

Amy smiled. "Thanks. It is nice to have less to worry about."

"Don't forget, dear, you need to visit Misha's brother, the Abbot. It's the right thing to do, to give your condolences. Never know when we might need the Abbot."

CHAPTER EIGHT

To Babelsberg

As the road curved through a forest and into Potsdam, Amy discovered that Thoren was both a driver and a travel guide on the local area. Slim and blond, wearing a wool jacket, he looked like the typical well-heeled German.

"We are following the Havel River, which flows into the Elbe River. The rivers all flow to the Baltic Sea. Even our lakes with canals form waterways to the north coast and run into the Baltic." He went on to say that the largest lake was Lake Schwerin, where the Stör River flowed into the Elbe. "A sixteenth-century canal called the Wallensteingraben connects the lake with the Baltic Sea at Wismar."

"How deep is the lake?" asked Amy.

"Very deep. In feet, over one hundred seventy feet."

Amy was impressed and said so.

Thoren went on to say that this was nothing. In Austria's Lake Toplitz, the depth was over three hundred feet.

The lake is deep, cold, and very likely has crevices. The treasure could hide anywhere, thought Amy.

"Where have I heard that lake's name?"

Again, Thoren was full of information. "Over the decades, Lake Toplitz has been a prime spot for searches and often in the news. No treasure seeker thinks it has given up all it holds. Many believe it is where the Nazis hid their gold."

He laughed. "And hidden, it is. At least four have died in that lake trying to find the gold. They found counterfeit British banknotes and printing presses—but no gold. Still, gold hunters keep at it."

Within minutes, they were on a street in Potsdam, looking for the film archives but seeing only the immense, eighteenth-century palace of Frederick the Great, Schloss Sanssouci, and the Schloss Cecilienhof, the latter being the site of the 1945 Potsdam Conference. She asked if Thoren or his brother had ever been to the archives and again was surprised by his answer. It seemed Frederic was a film buff and particularly liked old movies. He researched his thesis at the film archives when he was at the university.

Amy couldn't believe what Thoren said next. His brother's thesis was on Nazi gold—*Raubgold*, he called it. When she asked if she could read it, Thoren said that a copy of the thesis was at his mother's house.

"*Ja*, we can pick it up on the way back to Berlin. My mother will be pleased that someone is interested in it. She never understood why he spent so much time absorbed in films. Today, Frederic works in South Africa for an investment company."

Amy had to ask why the film archives had information on Nazi gold, but Thoren wasn't sure. "I was not a student like my brother, but Miss Prowers, stories are told all over this area about the Nazi gold. I grew up surrounded by rumors, theories on what happened to the gold. That is how I know about the searches at Lake Toplitz."

Thoren went on to say that he had no idea Amy and Sonora were interested in Nazi gold. Amy had to laugh. "We weren't until I went to Vilnius. Now, we're into the search. So, what has been said about the gold all these years?"

Thoren told her that many Germans were sure the gold was somewhere in the country. "Every few years, another group develops a theory that is a bust. Frederic always said that no good could come from finding the gold. But he never would say why."

The road turned away from the famous palaces and headed for Babelsberg. Thoren knew the area and found parking near the library and archives.

"Come with me," said Amy. "It's very likely that I'll need some help with the German language."

The office manager, a tall, heavyset man, apologized, saying the archives were in the process of being computerized. The present system consisted of paper files. After looking up indexes for Nazi gold, Nazi money, banks, and gold reserves in banks, they found one bit of information that was a summary of what gold had been found so far.

Amy was surprised to see that the information was in the *Guinness Book of Records*, which called the Nazis' looting of gold the greatest robbery in the history of the world. She sat down in one of the library chairs and told Thoren she would read this translation in German; he continued to flip through the paper files.

She read that one of the ways in which the Nazis financed the war was by looting the gold reserves of the countries they conquered. Additionally, they melted down the gold of the Holocaust victims and cast it into bars bearing the mark of the German central bank, the Reichsbank. Much of the gold was spent on the war, but a question had always remained about how much was left at the end of the war.

According to the article, the most famous finding was the Merkers mine, a salt mine some two hundred miles south of Berlin. There, much of the Reichsbank gold had been hidden, along with many art treasures, some from German museums and others looted from conquered nations.

Amy skipped over the description of the artwork—not because she thought it wasn't important but because the library didn't have a copy machine. She had to commit to memory or to notes what she was reading, and that meant focusing on details related to the gold.

And nothing has been found today, thought Amy as Thoren handed her another article on some of the gold chases that had taken place in Germany. One search was on Lake Walchensee, one of the deepest lakes in Bavaria. But nothing was ever found there.

Another lake was the one in Austria, Lake Toplitz, that Thoren had mentioned. For decades, it had been a site of searches, often resulting in the deaths of divers. All they ever found were forged British banknotes and printing presses.

She looked up as Thoren finished his files. According to Thoren, a different treasure search was going on for the Amber Room, the treasure taken from Russia and Catherine's Palace at Tsarskoye Selo south of St. Petersburg.

"Oh, no," said Amy. "I can only manage one treasure at a time." She laughed and handed him the papers to be filed again in the archives. "We're close, Thoren, but no cigar. I have a feeling something has been left out. We may have just missed it. Let's see if your brother's thesis gives us any more leads."

As they left the complex, the office manager picked up the phone to call a private number to an estate outside Vienna. "Sir, the Prowers family is looking for the gold. Thought you would like to know."

CHAPTER NINE

Back from Babelsberg

The sun was sinking in the western sky as they drove back to Berlin. Amy watched a flock of geese in a V formation, heading south. Winter was on the way.

They crossed a small creek and then the Havel River, which flowed north, emptying into the Elbe River. Amy was struck by the number of waterways north of Berlin.

If I had been a Nazi during World War II, she thought, *why would I take the gold south? North was the Baltic Sea and the North Sea—both much closer than landlocked Bavaria and Switzerland.*

In her mind, she saw a map of Germany. Hamburg was where the Elbe River flowed into the North Sea. Toward the end of World War II, that route would have been too dangerous. The Allies were waiting for any ship coming out of Germany.

North of Berlin was the Baltic Sea. True, the ship or the submarine would have to circle Denmark, but once the ship was in the North Sea, it would be looking at the North Atlantic, a body of water large enough to provide an escape route.

Why do I think ships?

The reason was obvious. Gold bullion was heavy, which meant they had to use ships for transportation out of Europe.

No other way seems viable.

To her, using ships was a no-brainer because of the weight of the bullion. No other means except water could transport such a heavy load out of Germany.

"Do these little creeks and rivers go north to the Baltic or empty into the North Sea?" she asked Thoren.

"*Ja*. The Elbe River goes to the North Sea through Hamburg. Others go to the Baltic, connected by canals."

"Leave it to the Germans. If you can't get from here to there, build a canal to connect you. Quite brilliant," said Amy.

"Oh, no," Thoren interrupted. They were stopped dead in traffic. He turned on the Mercedes's navigation system. "A demonstration is up ahead." He picked up his phone and read the text. "The demonstration is some right-wing, neo-Nazi group. I think I can avoid them." Thoren pulled into the right lane and followed a stream of cars with the same idea of looking for a detour.

"What are they protesting?" asked Amy.

"Who knows? We have many so-called right-wing groups today in Germany. We have a protest a month, but none are publicized. They do not want left-wingers trying to stop them. It is a show to the general population that they are still around. Did you know it is a crime to mention the word *Nazi* in Germany?"

He told her the detour would take them near his mother's house. "I am going to call and see if she is home. We can pick up the thesis."

"Sounds like a plan."

Amy was pleased. The thesis had been completed a decade ago but might have something of interest that had not been obvious to his brother Frederic at the time.

She had found nothing of real interest in the film library, but the drive up and back had given her a view of the waterways and how they might have been used to transport the gold. If the bullion never left Germany, then the Nazis could have hidden it somewhere north of Berlin, very likely near a river or a canal. Amy knew she needed a good map—better than the one in her head.

"I cannot get my mother to pick up the phone, but the house is only a few blocks away," said Thoren.

The neighborhood was quiet and neat. Each house had a small fence and an enclosed, small yard with flowers or vegetables.

"What is happening?" Thoren almost shouted as he slowed to let a police car pass by. They rounded the corner and saw two more police cars stopped in front of a house. "That is my mother's house."

He pulled up to the curb and leaned out of the car. One of the police officers stopped him. They spoke for a moment, and then Thoren went into the house. The police officer walked over to Amy, who was sitting in the Mercedes.

Now was the time to practice her German. But as she opened her mouth, she realized the police officer was speaking to her in very good English.

"It is a break-in. We think a robbery, but only one room was destroyed. I guess you would say trashed."

Their conversation was interrupted by another police officer. Amy was able to follow the gist of the conversation, and it seemed they were about ready to leave. Then, the first police officer turned to her and, in perfect English, told her she could go into the house. She thanked him and headed inside, unsure what was going on but wanting to help if she could.

Thoren's mother was sitting on a couch. "Thank you for coming. I am Julia," she said.

His mother's English was perfect, and Amy was beginning to wonder if everyone in Germany was bilingual.

"I am pleased to meet you. Your aunt has been so kind to Thoren. May I offer you a cup of coffee? Whoever broke in only messed up Frederic's room. He is my son who is in South Africa."

While Julia poured coffee, Thoren and Amy headed to the room that was trashed. The furnishings were simple: a bed, a dresser, a small desk, and a bookcase. All the drawers were open, and the contents of the bookcase were scattered on the floor.

"Amy, the only thing missing is Frederic's thesis. It was sitting on the bottom shelf. Why would someone take it?" Thoren turned to her, looking puzzled.

She thought for a moment. "When we were at the film library, did we mention the thesis? I think we did. We talked about it in the car before we arrived."

He picked up her point. "Either the car is bugged, or someone overheard us in the archive room."

"I think it's the car. My aunt's car would be a target for any number of industrial spies. Most of them would be interested in her business with the Committee. Only you and I know Sonora doesn't do business in the car."

"You are right, Amy. I will see if I can find a bug."

He left to go out to the car. She sat down with his mother for a cup of coffee.

"This is great coffee, and I'm a coffeeholic," said Amy.

"It is Kenyan. My son Frederic sends it to me from South Africa, of all places. Would you like another cup?"

"Yes, please."

As the elderly lady poured coffee, she recalled that Frederic had a safe-deposit box at the bank. "Amy, I have the key. Before Frederic left, he took me to the bank, and I signed on to access the box. He told me he kept his notes in the box. Do you think the notes could help?"

"I'm sure they could."

Amy listened while Julia talked about Frederic, who was obsessed with the new Nazi parties cropping up all over the world. "He was excited about his job managing and selling securities but worried that South Africa was full of Nazis—or so it seemed to him." She looked at Amy. "He promised me he would be careful. Best of all, one day, the company will transfer him back to

Germany. I pray every day for his return. Ah, here is the key. I keep it on my key ring."

"I can't speak for my aunt," said Amy, "but Lliessle Bank needs advisors. Maybe he could work for her."

"I would not want you to ask for us, Amy. We are so glad that Thoren works for Mrs. Lliessle. She has done so much for him. We could not ask her for more."

Amy understood the old lady's reluctance to push a job for another son. But being Sonora's niece, she could ask, and she said so.

"Let's see what can be worked out."

"Thank you, Amy. Whatever happens, thank you."

Amy sipped the coffee; the taste was full-bodied and smooth. She thought about the key. If it was ever lost, then the signature at the bank was what mattered. She looked out the window at Thoren, who was still checking the car.

"Can we go to the bank now?"

"Ah, no," said Julia. "Closed for the day. And I will go to my sister's house for the night—or until the locksmith has repaired the door. I would stay in the neighborhood, but my children will not hear of it. Tomorrow is Thoren's day off, and we will go to the bank then."

She looked at Amy conspiratorially. "I know I am a signatory on the safe-deposit box. I have signature authority on all of Frederic's accounts, and so does Thoren. I never asked Frederic how he did it. He was so smart about banking laws."

"Perfect," said Amy as Thoren came back into the house.

What she was really thinking was, *What could be in the accounts and boxes that require all the signatures? Did Frederic suspect his days were numbered?*

Thoren looked at Amy and rolled his eyes. Had he found something? Amy realized Thoren might have found a bug but hadn't been able to remove it. She made small talk as they stopped at Thoren's aunt's home to drop off Julia.

"What a day!" Amy chatted on about the film archives as they made their way to Sonora's house in Berlin.

The iron gates in front of the Lliessle Estate opened slowly. Thoren drove up the drive and parked in front of the mansion. He got out of the car and walked to the center of the front yard.

"I am paranoid because I found a bug in the car. You probably figured that out, but I cannot remove it."

"Don't worry. Sonora will put her security people to work figuring out how to remove the bug and who put it in the car."

• • •

Sonora was not pleased.

"Security is researching where the bug is sold. Apparently, it's high-tech and not something you can buy at any electronics store."

Amy quickly explained how she and Thoren were discussing his brother's thesis while they drove back to Berlin. "I'm sure someone got ahead of us and stole it from his mother's house before we got there. We may have mentioned the thesis at the archives, where someone could have overheard us. Is this another so-called coincidence?"

Sonora pointed out that everything about the map and the journal was a coincidence, starting with the way in which Vince found them.

"Thoren, you're going with your mother tomorrow to find whatever your brother may have left in the box. I want one of my security staff to go with you. Whoever thinks your brother had information could be watching and might try to take it from you. I don't want that to happen. I want to know what's in Frederic's safe-deposit box. I hope your mother will understand about all the fuss."

"Right."

Sonora wasn't finished. "You'd think it was ridiculous someone would want his thesis, written a decade ago. But I recall that Frederic was one of the foremost experts on Nazi gold. He was out of the country when Vince needed help.

"Besides, everyone thought Frederic was a neo-Nazi, a disguise he loved. He openly said he was in the neo-Nazi movement. But I know he hated right-wingers and neo-Nazi organizations. He also gave financial advice to the Lliessle Bank's branch in Berlin."

She paused. "Amy, he looked at me and said, 'If you are one of them in the beginning, they trust you.' I think he was telling me he was a plant. Though I have no idea for who. Maybe just for himself as a way to vindicate the past."

Amy and Sonora looked at each other, realizing how little they really did know.

"For once, Sonora, I'm glad you have a good security service."

Sonora laughed. "We can thank the Count, who must be cheering in his grave over our use of the service. I wish you would stay here, but I know how you like the Adlon Kempinski."

Amy smiled. "It's my favorite hotel—or, should I say, apartment. Ace likes it too but always stays in a room in the regular part of the hotel. After all, the hotel is in the center of Berlin."

Thoren interrupted them. "I just got a call from my aunt. My mother was admitted to the hospital for indigestion or a possible stroke. We have to delay going to Frederic's safe-deposit box."

CHAPTER TEN

The Adlon-Kempinski Hotel

Wolfgang had just spent another day drinking coffee in the small restaurant across from Berlin's Adlon Kempinski Hotel. The owner of the restaurant was a member of the Grey Eagles. He let Wolfgang sit in the shop all day if he had to, no questions asked. His demeanor was not threatening. And his expensive but casual clothes made him almost invisible.

He didn't have to wait long. Marton's information was spot-on. A taxi pulled up, and Amy got out and entered the hotel. He knew she stayed at the family apartment, not at her aunt's home, so following her should be easy.

That evening, Amy had never been more pleased to have her own apartment at the Kempinski. Her father bought the apartment after the Berlin Wall came down, in part because he liked the hotel's service, something Amy agreed was superb. The hotel was in the heart of Berlin yet had an atmosphere of privacy that she never felt in Sonora's mansion.

Sonora's house was huge but like a hotel, with people coming and going. Usually, they were Committee members, but her aunt also had a social schedule. Right now, her aunt's private security service was combing the home, the grounds, and the vehicles for eavesdropping devices. The bug Thoren found had set off a frenzied search for other devices.

From the apartment, she looked out on the western end of Unter den Linden, the most famous boulevard in central Berlin. The sun had nearly set, and the lights on the Brandenburg Gate were slowly coming on. To the north, she could see the Reichstag, the German parliament building. She loved the view and thought of how the boulevard must have looked a hundred years ago when linden trees lined the bridle path. Today, eighteenth-century buildings sat like citadels along the street.

Not many people were out walking. The wind had blown in from the North Sea, and a cold fall night kept the walkers and sightseers inside. One exception was the man sitting outside the coffee shop across the boulevard.

Amy watched as he poured coffee out of a pot and lit a cigarette. Why did he look familiar? It wasn't his face; it was the gray jacket he was wearing. The jacket looked as if it belonged in a grand prix race, not at a coffee shop.

She had seen a jacket like that the other day in the archives. At the table next to where she and Thoren were working, a man was wearing a similar jacket. The streets of Berlin had a lot of jackets, but not ones that color or with the three black stripes on the sleeve.

Staring at the man out the window, she saw nothing else unusual.

I'm being paranoid. The monk being killed is making me crazy, she thought.

The ringing of the hotel phone startled her. The caller identified himself as the Abbot of St. Benedict's Monastery. She realized he was Misha's brother.

"Very sorry, Miss Prowers, to bother you at your apartment, but I need to speak to you if possible. Your aunt told me you're here."

Amy's style was not to meet a stranger on the spur of the moment, but Sonora wanted her to meet the Abbot. Besides, he was Misha's brother, and she felt a kinship to the elderly monk, who had tried to help her before he was killed.

She was hungry, and nothing could be safer than meeting in one of the hotel restaurants. Thinking about her options, she chose the two-star Michelin Lorenz Adlon Esszimmer, a favorite of Sonora's. Not only did the restaurant have a view of the Brandenburg Gate and Unter den Linden, but the menu also featured regional cuisine. One of her favorite dishes, *Berliner Currywurst*, was always served. The Abbot accepted her invitation to meet in the Adlon Esszimmer.

"I'm wearing a navy-blue pantsuit. I'll make the reservation for in an hour. Does that work for you?"

"Yes, I know the restaurant. Thank you, Miss Prowers." He didn't add that he knew what she looked like. He had seen several pictures of her at Sonora's home.

CHAPTER ELEVEN

Dinner at the Kempinski Hotel

To Amy, one of the benefits of living at the Kempinski was that the staff treated her as part of their family. She was seated immediately and told the maître d' she was expecting a gentleman and would order when he arrived.

"While I wait, I'll have a double vodka, chilled, and make it a high-end Russian vodka."

She looked out the window at Unter den Linden with the lights on along the boulevard. People were passing by the windows of the restaurant. The one exception was the man standing on the corner, smoking a cigarette. He looked familiar, and she knew why. He was the same man, wearing a gray jacket and a matching cap, she had seen sitting in the coffeehouse across the street.

At least he was outside, and she was inside on this cold November day. The city lights on Unter der Linden flickered brightly beneath gray skies in the encroaching cold. The city was exhausted after the beer fests, and most Germans began to stay inside and prepare for winter and the holidays.

I love the cold, drippy fog, she thought. *The preference for cold weather must be in the Prowers's genes.*

Ace had emailed her that the delays for security alerts were over and that he was finally on a flight to Berlin. He said he wanted to return to a city with culture. She was sure he was fed up with his Arabian Peninsula assignment because he added he had enough of the sun—and sand.

She looked down the multilane boulevard. From the Brandenburg Gate down Unter der Linden, Amy could see a street lined with history. The first building, the Neue Wache, was a guardhouse, an example of German Greek Revival architecture. She knew it was built in 1816 by the crown prince of Prussia, and it had been used as a war memorial for the victims of war and dictatorship since 1931.

Farther on, in her mind's eye, she saw the Berlin State Opera, St. Hedwig's Cathedral, and the Berlin State Library, founded in 1661. She remembered seeing the buildings during visits to Berlin in the early 1970s, when the wall had still been in place. The Russian and Italian embassies were both huge concrete edifices, with their architecture from the nineteenth century. They were bombed during the war but reconstructed to look like they did before the war.

Her father told her how the street had been a pile of rubble after World War II. When she first visited Berlin, she remembered, the hotel was behind the Berlin Wall. Now, the boulevard had been rebuilt. The renovations gave her a feeling of progress but without a loss of history. She planned to enjoy the museums; she never could visit them often enough. Until 1989, they had been behind the wall that divided Berlin for nearly thirty years.

Her waiter saw her looking at the boulevard. He spoke in passable English. "Much changed over the years in what was East Berlin. Was never like the fancy designer stores on the Kurfürstendamm," he said. "The street today looks like it did when the Russians ran Berlin."

He paused, then told her he was glad the wall was down but that the old Stasi, East German spies, were still living in these houses. "They just"—and he moved his hands in a gesture— "go back into a wall we cannot see. I tell you, miss, they still live here."

"*Ich kenne*," Amy said in German. She was pleased she could say "I know" in German.

She sipped her vodka. Even inside the restaurant, she felt the pull of the foggy mist that had settled on the city. Somehow, it was comforting. But she knew she had to leave the city and head north. It was time to start looking for the gold.

The Abbot had been living at the monastery before the Russians had put up the wall in 1961, when it was East Berlin, and he still lived there when the wall came down in 1989. Because of what Misha had told her about the gold, the Abbot probably knew even more. But would he share it with her?

Before she knew it, the Abbot was being seated. He was very tall, with his robes hanging evenly over his body, and he looked much younger than Misha.

After introductions, they both ordered the specialty: *Berliner Currywurst*, a small sausage with a tomato sauce, and *Gebackener Hecht*, baked pike. She picked out a moderately priced Bockstein Riesling from the Mosel River Valley.

"A drink while we wait?" she asked.

The Abbot said, "Vodka, straight up."

She looked at the waiter. "Make it two doubles." To the Abbot, she asked, "Is Russian vodka all right?"

He nodded and said, "Thank you for meeting with me on such short notice."

"No problem. I'm sorry for the loss of your brother."

He nodded again. "I miss him. He knew the risks all the years he lived in Vilnius. Now, he is in God's hands."

She hesitated, then asked, "The risks?"

"Vilnius is known for its criminal elements. Not a place for a monk."

To Amy, his response sounded logical—almost *too* logical.

"Meeting Misha meant a lot to me. He was one of the last people to talk to my husband before he left for Pakistan. I thought he might know what Vince was doing. When I saw him, he told me the Nazi gold, the *Raubgold*, was what I should try to find because that was what Vince was hunting."

She paused. "I know it's been twenty years since Vince died. Those years passed with none of us bothering about his search to find the gold. Now, I'm going to finish his quest. Most of the gold hasn't been found. I think it's here, in Germany."

The Abbot knew what she wanted: clues to find the Nazi gold. It seemed that every organization out there was searching for it.

"Obviously, you do not believe the gold went to South America or is hidden in Austria."

"No."

Amy sounded positive, which told him she knew more about Vince's search than he realized.

"How did Vince find the journal?" The Abbot knew the story from Misha, but he wanted to hear Amy's version.

More than twenty years had passed, but in her mind, the event was as clear as yesterday. She spoke quickly, repeating what she assumed he must already know.

She told the Abbot that Vince, whom she had known most of her life, had been born with a calm demeanor. Even after surviving a plane crash, he didn't appear to be too stressed. She was the one who was upset. Vince's response to the crash was to drink most of a bottle of single malt scotch from the Isle of Islay, and to go to bed.

The next day, as the investigation into the crash proceeded, he told her about finding the box in the woods. When he landed in a small forest, his feet hit some type of steel case. Ignoring it, he rolled up his parachute and walked out of the woods.

Fate, he thought, had parachuted him on top of it. She remembered being surprised he didn't mention the box to the rescue crew, keeping it a secret from the military. No one, apparently, went into the woods to see where his feet hit the ground.

Curious about what might be in the box, he returned to find it. She had gotten into the spirit of the search and went with him. As they entered the woods, her first look led her to conclude that they would never find the box. It was England, but this woodland was no street in London. Instead, it was a forest straight out of the time of Henry VIII. The trees were thick, and the vegetation was overgrown. But Vince said he had landed in a small, open space.

They found a trail through the trees that deer and foxes probably used. As they followed it, Vince's photographic memory served him well. He walked almost directly to the open area and started moving weeds and tall grass around. Even today, Amy thought Vince was right—that fate had led them to find the box because of the ease with which they found it.

She looked at the Abbot. "That's how it began. I need you to help me."

The Abbot understood that she was determined to find the gold. How could he dissuade her or divert her? Maybe he couldn't.

They looked at each other, thinking of how much gold was waiting to be found. The subject changed when the waiter arrived with the wine.

"You must know those of us who work at St. Benedict's Monastery appreciate the support of your aunt."

Amy didn't know how much her aunt donated but smiled as if she did. She had finished her double vodka, as had the Abbot.

"Would you like another? A double shot?"

"Nothing better than Russian vodka."

Amy motioned to the waiter for another round of vodka, wondering how the Abbot had acquired a taste for Russian vodka. She wasn't going to mention the map, nor had she told Misha about it.

"My departed husband had many secrets. The box he landed on when he parachuted out of his burning plane contained a journal. He translated the journal as best he could. After he died, Sonora and I never found it in any of his papers or safe-deposit boxes. We believed the journal was destroyed when he died in Pakistan."

Amy explained how a week ago, she had found the journal hidden behind a wall in her home in Colorado. An avalanche had destroyed the wall, revealing the bag. Besides neglecting to tell him about the map, she also neglected to tell him that all the notations on the map were in northern Germany. Why should she tell him everything until she knew what he wanted?

The Abbot looked at Amy, knowing that he had to bring Marton into the discussion. If she didn't know about Marton's association with the neo-Nazi movements, then he had to tell her. That was a problem when dealing with a *blénder.* He couldn't tell which side Marton was on.

"Amy, Marton did some translations for Vince. But today, he is a neo-Nazi and a member of the National Democratic Party, as the majority group calls itself. He is one of the leaders."

"Marton's father worked for Count Lliessle for years in Switzerland, and because of that association, Sonora trusts him," said Amy. She surprised him by saying, "I looked up Nazi organizations on the internet." She paused, realizing how long she had ignored the neo-Nazi groups, while Vince, her father, and Sonora were often obsessing over them. "Never did I realize how many groups existed. I always knew using the word *Nazi* was illegal in Germany. Never thought about right-wing groups being Nazis by another name. What purpose do they have in today's world?"

According to the Abbot, the groups in Germany operated by calling themselves nationalists and never using the word *Nazi* or *Hitler* outside their membership meetings. They claimed to care about the Fatherland and didn't like the type of state Germany had become, with all the immigrants. They wanted to build a new Germany for the German people.

"Some of the supporters of the movement are the last citizens you would expect to join, and all of the sections of German society belong to the groups. They are soft-spoken, are taught to sound patriotic and to deny in public their affiliation. Still, police and journalists shadow them, hoping for a story or for an arrest."

The Abbot was watching Amy, who was looking out the window at the man talking on his cell phone. For some reason, the man on the street seemed to make her nervous.

"You're saying that Marton is one of those people?" she asked.

"Yes, but his activities are not silent. Did you know that he made a visit to Paraguay? That is an odd trip for a museum curator to take. It is not London, nor New York, nor Paris, where there are museums."

According to the Abbot, the neo-Nazi movement had been active since World War II. Some people, not only in Germany but around the world, wanted to revive Nazi beliefs. Many European countries had enacted laws that made Nazi symbols and beliefs illegal. Nazi groups then renamed themselves and went underground.

Austria, Russia, France, Sweden, Belgium, and the United States had organizations that were part of a global network. The aim of these groups was to fight for the Nazi political agenda, which was racist. They believed that Aryans were the master race, denied the Holocaust, and warned that the extinction of the German people was imminent.

"Amy, they used to be called *Steifelnazis*, 'Boot Nazis.' Now, they are called *Kravattennazis*, 'Tie Nazis.' They use social media. They hold mini-protests, especially in university cities, and then disappear into the night before the authorities show up. Not all, but many Germans feel they are second-class citizens of the world, living with war guilt. I think that is an excuse."

As Amy listened, she realized she was beginning to understand the neo-Nazi movement and how it fit into contemporary society. She could see how the movement could become a way of life for the members.

"Abbot, why do they want to be separate? Is it to belong?"

He shrugged. "Who knows? Maybe all of the Nazis killed in World War II have been reincarnated in another life, this life."

Amy laughed. "Your theory may not be as far-out as it sounds, though I hope those Nazis never return."

The conversation stopped as the waiter served the fish and poured the wine. They ate, making small talk about the history of the hotel and discussing who might have stayed in the Adlon

Kempinski since it opened in 1907. When he asked about the apartment, she told him how her father had bought it as the wall was coming down. The apartment was used by the family and business associates. According to Amy, it wasn't a real home—just a nice hotel suite they could always count on.

"The street is interesting to you?" asked the Abbot, as Amy kept looking out and each time seemed upset.

She moved her chair slightly. "Can you see the man standing outside on the street? Tell me if this guy in the gray jacket could be a neo-Nazi. I swear I've seen him or that jacket somewhere recently. He's been on this street and at the coffee shop across Unter den Linden since I checked in."

The Abbot leaned around the corner of the table to get a look. "Amy, it is his jacket. You have identified one of the Grey Eagles, the most prominent neo-Nazi organization in Berlin."

"The jacket reminds me of those Formula One racing jackets," said Amy.

He told her that was how the Grey Eagles had designed the jacket. They wanted those outside the group not to see the jacket as a symbol.

"I saw one hanging over the back of a chair when I was in the film archives in Potsdam."

"If you saw that jacket in Potsdam, you are probably being followed," said the Abbot. "You must have something they want."

Amy agreed immediately. "You're right. Someone put a bug on Sonora's car, the one Thoren was using to drive me around Berlin."

Now was the time to push his agenda. "What do you have that someone, a neo-Nazi, wants?"

"The journal Vince found? Why would they think I'd carry it around with me?"

"They may not think you know the importance of the journal. If it holds a key to the location of the gold bullion that was left in Germany at the end of World War II, nothing will keep them from looking for it."

The Abbot went on to say that he believed his brother Misha was killed because others thought he knew the location of the Nazi gold. The gold that had been in Vilnius and shipped out of the Czartoryski Estate.

"Misha thought that some of the gold had gone south with the Czartoryski family. The remainder, my brother was sure, was supposed to go out of northern Germany by freighter or by submarine. But it never did."

He leaned over to speak softly, though no one was at the adjacent table. "Misha told me that most of the bullion never left Germany. We both have contacts, Misha's in Vilnius and mine in Berlin, with neo-Nazi groups. They have been quietly but actively searching for the rest of the gold. Nazis always had detailed records, and that is why the journal could be so important to the search.

"The search is a frenzy to find the gold still in Germany or on the continent because after all these decades the gold shipped to other countries at the end of World War II has been spent. The members of these groups are not always employed, but they still need to have money to live and support their families."

The Abbot was sure that a map also existed. The men who hid the bullion were not just Nazis but Germans. Details, with copies in duplicate and triplicate, were part of the culture. He had to give Amy an opportunity to mention the map, if there was one.

"Marton has convinced the Grey Eagles that his father and Count Lliessle knew the location of the bullion after the war. He claims his long-dead father told him so," said the Abbot.

Amy knew that the map was important but changed the subject. Nothing had been said that would compel her to mention it. If the map was the key, then she and Sonora didn't see anything relevant on it. Neither Misha nor Marton spoke about a map. She would follow her dead husband's lead and not mention it to the Abbot.

"The problem is Sonora's relationship with Marton," said the Abbot.

Amy pointed out that Sonora was on the board of the Berlin Museum and regularly met with Marton on museum business.

"He is . . . how you say . . . well connected, and he visits old Nazis frequently. I told you that he went to Paraguay and was back in four days, barely long enough to get over jet lag. Does your aunt know about these trips?"

Amy didn't hesitate. "If she doesn't, I'll tell her."

The waiter arrived to clear the table and then brought them both espressos. They were too full for dessert. Amy asked the waiter if he had ever seen the man who had been standing outside on Unter den Linden.

He surprised Amy and the Abbot by saying, "Our security service just detained a man wearing the same type of gray racing jacket."

Amy put down her espresso cup. "What did he do?"

"I was told the man was up on a floor, trying to break into a room. The hotel has security cameras, and he was picked up before he broke in."

"What floor?"

"The third."

Amy looked at the Abbot. "My family's apartment is on the third floor."

He shrugged. "Probably a coincidence, and I would not put much importance on it. No rooms were broken into, right?" The Abbot looked at the waiter.

"Yes."

"So, Amy, no harm is done."

Amy was glad she had finished dinner because her appetite was gone. The Abbot had been very flippant over the floor the intruder was on. She didn't feel the same. Her apartment was only a hotel room with nothing personal in it. Copies of the journal and the map were at Sonora's. Sonora had put the real ones in her bank safe-deposit box.

The Abbot made small talk about the beauty of Berlin in the evening lights. Then, as if he could hear their discussion, the man outside put his cell phone in his pocket and walked down Unter den Linden to the east and out of sight.

As they ordered another cup of espresso, the director of security for the hotel arrived at their table, requesting to speak to her. Amy agreed to meet him in a few minutes when she finished her coffee.

She and the Abbot said goodbye in the lobby.

"I promise to be in touch if something comes up on the gold bullion," said Amy.

"Give me a call, and we can have dinner again. Maybe your aunt can join us. I always enjoy her points of view."

Amy had to laugh and felt compelled for some reason, maybe because he was a monk, to share her feelings. "She does have a perspective. I'm never sure if it's hers, the Committee's, or my grandfather's—and he's been dead for decades."

The Abbot turned and watched Amy and the security director walk down a corridor off the lobby. He knew that the attempt to get into her apartment had failed. The man in the gray jacket had been caught by a security camera, and he was picked up by hotel security.

The attempt had not been a complete failure. Now, he knew that the journal was stored elsewhere. If Sonora had the journal and the map, then finding them would be difficult. It wasn't as if a thief could search her home. Maybe he didn't have to find them. All he had to do was get Sonora or Amy to talk about the map.

A strategy was something he would plot later. Now, he had to get a German official in the Berlin police department to call the security director and get one of the Grey Eagles out of custody. The other Grey Eagle should be just down Unter den Linden at a tavern.

• • •

Amy and the security director looked at the hotel tapes. She could see the man in the Grey Eagles jacket trying to open the door to her hotel room. When he couldn't open it, he checked his phone.

"He wanted to be sure he had your room number," said the director. "Watch him try again."

The man tried again, but he still couldn't open the door.

"Who is this guy?" wondered Amy. "I've never seen him before."

"Probably a common criminal who does not know that we have special locks on the floor where the long-term guests stay," said the director. "The criminals do not know that it takes more than a screwdriver to pop these locks."

Amy felt a little more secure but asked the director to escort her to the apartment. He checked inside, just to be sure no one was in the apartment. His phone buzzed.

"My men have finished their sweep of the hotel room, and extra guards are on your wing."

Inside her apartment, Amy pondered what to do next. If Sonora knew what had happened, then her aunt would insist that she move to her house in the Berlin suburbs. Living downtown was more interesting, and only this brush with the Grey Eagles made it dangerous. No one could say that the group wouldn't invade Sonora's home, though such a move would be unlikely, considering Sonora's armed security force. But then, someone *did* bug her house and her cars.

Tomorrow, she decided, after Ace arrived, they would go to Sonora's house for lunch and find out what was happening with Thoren and his mother.

Thinking of Ace, she pulled a map of northern Germany out of the desk drawer. Thanks to her father, there was a map of every European country in the desk. This one detailed roads, rivers, canals, and towns. It was a map that could be bought in any store. She looked at the map. In his own way, Misha had been trying to tell her to go north.

The Nazis must have planned to take the gold out by ship. The question was how to get the bullion to the Baltic Sea. It could have been hidden along the route. If so, then it was very likely that it was still there. The Allies were bombing the ports, so the bullion would not have been stored at ports. She ignored the possibility that the gold had made it to one of the ports on the Baltic Sea and was at the bottom of the ocean in a bombed-out freighter or in a sunken submarine.

Looking at the map, she realized that she was wrong about the Havel River being the main route north. The Havel River fed into the Elbe River, the main water route to Hamburg. No way did the Nazis take the gold to Hamburg. The city was a port on the North Sea, where the Allied ships had to be watching and stopping all freighter traffic.

The Elbe River flowed north but was linked to the Schweiner See, a large lake by a canal. The lake was connected to the Baltic Sea at Wismar by the Wallenstein, a sixteenth-century canal.

Where along this route could the gold bullion be hidden? On that point, she had no clue. Once she told Ace what she believed the route to be, he might have some insight as to where the Nazis would have hidden their treasure. Thoren also might have a theory once they reviewed his brother's papers from the safe-deposit box.

Looking at the map again, she saw the importance of Wismar. With a bay and a dock that allowed large steamers to unload, the city was a key manufacturing center for iron, paper, and machinery.

She got up and went to a row of books, thankful that her father had stocked up on so many references on Germany in English. She opened one and read that historically, Wismar was part of the Hanseatic League, a federation of northern German towns and cities formed in the twelfth century to facilitate trade, and also part of Sweden. In 1903, Sweden relinquished its rights.

During World War II, the city had airplane and railway factories, and it was damaged by Allied air raids. After the war, the city was part of the Soviet Occupation Zone. In 2002, with its brick Gothic buildings, the city was listed as a United Nations Educational Scientific and Cultural Organization World Heritage Site. According to the write-up, the town center was one of the largest marketplaces in northern Germany.

To Amy, hiding the gold in what was a tourist town didn't seem logical. She looked back at the map. A safer place to hide the bullion was along the waterways south of Wismar. Unless, and it was always a possibility, the gold left on a ship that was sunk at sea. If that was true, then why were the Nazis looking for it today?

Since most of the original Nazis were no longer alive, the neo-Nazis would have no idea if the gold was lost. And why were the Bank of England officials who died in the plane crash in England carrying a map supposedly showing where it was? Nope, the gold was still up there.

She and Sonora often kidded Ace about his map-reading ability. He called himself a professional. His Special Forces training made him not only an expert shot but also an expert at map reading. To Amy, map reading seemed like common sense. Tomorrow, he would read the map, and they would learn if the story had another ending.

. . .

The next morning, Amy was at Sonora's, waiting for Ace, who was late as usual. He had an excuse this time. His flight was delayed again. While she waited, Amy decided to do some research on the computer in her aunt's home.

Sonora was in her office, meeting with her security staff. She was not happy about the bug in her car and wanted to be sure that the other vehicles, as well as her home, were clean. Amy knew that a detailed sweep would be made. They might validate that the house and cars were clean, but she doubted that they'd find who did it.

Turning back to the computer, she started searching neo-Nazi websites. She immediately saw that the scope was too broad for that search. She had no idea that so many neo-Nazi groups had sprung up in Germany—and all over the world as well.

Numerous articles were about right-wing extremists, which were really today's Nazis. The term was collective—generally indicating antidemocratic, pro-authoritarian philosophies, ethnopluralism, or racism—and had been used by right-wing extremists since the 1970s in response to the term *liberal multiculturalism*. A multicultural society, the integration of people of different origins, had no place with right-wing extremists. Another belief was that elites were obligated to understand politics for the masses.

Amy sat back and thought for a moment. That statement could be made about her aunt and the Committee. The Committee made decisions it considered best for the masses, but it wasn't racist. At least, she didn't think so. When she started attending meetings, she would find out.

She turned back to the computer and did some more research. Apparently, governments sanctioned right-wing extremists differently. Germany's sanctions were against right-wing groups. Austria and Switzerland had no sanctions.

Complicated was the only word Amy could think of as she finally ended the computer search. One significant point occurred to her; with all those groups, which had to include many leaders who had oversized egos, they must be hopelessly splintered. At least for today, that was good news for local governments. Maybe it was even good for her search. Now, where was Ace?

CHAPTER TWELVE

Nuremberg

The Crescent Boar—one of Nuremberg's most popular places
to eat and drink—was, as usual, crowded. Marton scanned the
room, looking for Pedro Czartoryski. He hadn't seen Pedro
Czartoryski since they were schoolboys together in East Berlin.
In those days, everyone thought they were brothers.

Pedro saw him and waved him over to the bar. Marton
thought his friend had barely aged. He had the same thin,
dark-brown hair, combed over to the side. What was new was a
small moustache. That addition probably was because his father,
Bazyli, had a large black one.

"Marton, my old friend, you have not changed a bit." Pedro
motioned to the bartender for two drafts of beer. Beers in hand,
they moved to a table in a quiet corner.

Pedro flicked his head to the side, and Marton's eyes followed. Their minder was sitting in a booth on the other side of the room. To Marton, minders always had the same look. He supposed it was part of their training in the BfV.

Marton got right to the point. Small talk wouldn't change the facts. "You think I have the old map Vince found. But I do not."

"We know your father had a copy," said Pedro, sipping his beer.

"You are right." Marton sounded frustrated. "My father and the Count came back from Switzerland over forty years ago with trunks of luggage. The map—or a copy, very likely—was with them. At that time, the Count bought the old nineteenth-century house in Berlin and rebuilt it as a fortress. The old man would be pleased that his wife lives there most of the year.

"My father got to know Sonora very well, as he spent his last years living in the guesthouse. He died a year after the Count. When Vince and Benton Prowers died, the map seemed to have disappeared."

Pedro shook his head. "Odds are the map is still at the estate. Only, no one knows for sure. As a banker, the Count would have put it in a safe-deposit box."

Marton thought for a moment. "Count Lliessle owned a private bank in Switzerland. They would never have trusted another Swiss bank. Or Vince might have given it to Amy. No one would have thought that she was interested in her husband's search. When Vince was alive, she was very involved with the Prowers' oil business. She would be the perfect cover, hiding in plain sight."

Pedro agreed that Marton had a point.

"But," said Marton, "the reason I came to Nuremberg was to research the files at the Documentation Center Museum. Even if I don't find anything, it will show Sonora I am serious. And besides, who knows what I will find."

"Is that the big building beside the old Nazi Party parade grounds?" asked Pedro.

"Right. During World War II, Nuremberg was bombed to the ground by the Allies. After the war, it was reconstructed using the original stone. In 1994, the city made the decision to establish the Documentation Center Museum. It was built as an extension of the Congress Hall, which was used by the Nazis for party rallies but never finished. Part of the historical significance is that it's right beside the old Nazi parade grounds. Today, it contains the most definitive history of the National Socialists, the Nazi Party."

Marton went on to say that a permanent exhibit called *Fascination and Terror* was on display in the museum, showing the history, causes, and consequences of the Nazi regime.

"What? You're kidding. Today's Germany named an exhibit *Fascination and Terror*?"

"It is no joke, Pedro. *Faszination und Gewalt*, a typical German title that talks about the fascination with violence. The Nazi Party rallies are shown on film, with an explanation of the fascination they held for the participants and for the people who watched them. The exhibit educates the people who see it by showing what led to the National Socialists' use of power and the consequences for the population."

For a moment, Pedro was silent. "The war ended in 1945, but the rally grounds and the stadium remain as they were then. The huge stadium, the Party Rally Grounds, today is empty. Yet, when I see it, I think that the ghosts are still alive," he said.

"Amazingly," said Marton, "between 1933 and 1938, the Nazis drew almost a million people to that stadium. The movie on the Nuremberg Trials made the stadium famous. The exhibit uses pictures and electronic display stations to make it easier for the younger generation to understand a very ugly history."

He wanted Pedro to understand his problem. "Pedro, the exhibit and records center was established in 1994, long after the war. I am counting on German efficiency to have put together all the records available on the war years."

Marton paused again, feeling frustrated. "If that fails, my fallback is the founding members of the education forum. Wealthy citizens donated funds to build the center. The Lliessle family was among the founders. I have a good relationship with Mrs. Lliessle. She knows me from my work at the Berlin Museum. I think she likes me. If I am careful and become part of the family, so to speak, I could find out what the family knows about the location of the gold."

Pedro laughed. "Good plan. If you find nothing at the documents center, go to Sonora Lliessle. All you have to do is have a good reason to be looking for the gold. 'Reparations' seems to be a buzzword everyone likes. You can say that you want to restore the gold to the victims."

Marton lifted his glass in a toast, and for the first time that day, he smiled. "In 1990, restoration groups received reparation payments from Swiss banks for relatives who died in the death camps. That is why I want to be quiet about what I find. I do not want the emphasis to be on more reparations. With any luck, while researching the documents, I will find references to the gold. Whoever finds the gold owns it."

Pedro agreed. "Even if you find a reference, the location of the bullion might not be listed."

"I should be so lucky," said Marton, who realized that he had been watching the crowd in the busy bar. Were they watching him and Pedro, or was he just seeing things? He turned back to Pedro.

"Years ago, my father told me he and the Count had documented all of their work. They saved their notes, written in an ancient Germanic language, in a journal so that only a trained translator could read them. While Sonora speaks passable German, she is not at a level to translate it. She will have to call me to translate the notes. I want to be able to tell her that my research at the document center is part of my work as a curator at the museum."

"And never mention the gold unless you have to," said Pedro before ordering another round of beer.

"Right. Now, what are you doing here?" asked Marton.

Pedro talked about the move that his family had made from Poland to Vienna to Nuremberg. "My father moved the mattress factory here to Nuremberg because it is a working man's town. The fact that it is home to neo-Nazis, right-wingers, whatever you want to call them, is an added benefit. My grandfather owned a large estate outside of Vienna. Today, my father thinks living there is more civilized. He is in town now to manage his business interests."

They both laughed.

Marton said that he had not expected Pedro's father, Bazyli Czartoryski, to ever be anything other than a committed Nazi. He looked around to be sure no one was in earshot. Their BfV minder was still at the other end of the tavern, sipping a large lager.

"Pedro, your father is beloved in Asuncion. They appreciate his support all of these years. Those men are anxious for us to find the gold. You and I have little to gain by finding it."

Pedro agreed. What could he and Marton do with all the gold?

"All I know, Marton, is that it is better for me to find it than the dozen or more groups in Germany looking for it. Thanks to the newspapers, I'm up-to-date on all of the searches for gold. The public loves hearing about the findings or non-findings."

Marton thought for a moment and said, "Mrs. Lliessle could be a big help. I will have to wait and see how she reacts to all of this. But Pedro, tell me, is our minder from the BfV? Is he following you or me?"

Pedro laughed. "It is very likely both of us."

Marton looked at his old friend Pedro. "Old Nazis, new Nazis, the Führer said the Reich would last a thousand years." As he spoke, both of them looked around the tavern. No one had heard his comment.

"Careful, my friend," said Pedro. "Someone might hear us. Right now, we only have one minder watching us, but you never know."

"Pedro, you cannot miss the guys who work for the BfV. Oh, sorry, the Federal Office for the Protection of the Constitution. Only the Russians have more innocuous titles. Are the guys who track the criminals any better?"

"Not really," said Pedro. "They all wear the same shoes. The Federal Criminal Police Office looks at narcotics, weapons, and financial crime. The office can overlap with the BfV because they also look at terrorists and crime motivated by politics. Remember to look at the shoes."

Pedro ordered two more beers. "You know my brother, Uwe. He is going to march tomorrow. Nothing for you to worry about. You will be at the documents center. The march will be another flash and splash."

"My God! Is that what they call it now?" said Marton.

"Yep. You may not know it, but the guys who wear the Grey Eagles jackets are hounded by the BfV, the government goons."

Pedro went on to say that tomorrow, the Grey Eagles would march for an hour through the center of town and the *Christkindlmarkt*. The plan was to fade into the alleyways before the authorities arrived.

"Uwe loves these marches."

"Your father loved marches, right?" asked Marton.

"That was in the old days. Today, his health keeps him from marching. You cannot be old and slow and march. He would be a liability. And it's not a special day. They pick the days at random. Remember, they want the publicity. That is what the march is all about."

Marton was not sure the marches were necessary. Obviously, the Grey Eagles felt differently. He wondered if protesting and marching were inspired by a Nazi gene. If so, then he didn't have it, and that was one reason why he wasn't a Nazi. But he had to pretend.

"The marches keep the police on their toes. Wish I could see it," Marton said.

Pedro understood. "Your job, Marton, is to find the gold. I still think the key to finding the gold is in the journal, the map, whatever Vince had. Or the clues are in the home in Berlin or in the Lliessle villas in Zurich."

Marton agreed. He looked back at the bar and saw that the lunch crowd had gone back to work. Only he, Pedro, and their minder were left in the bar. It was time to go.

"Thanks again for the use of the riverboat."

Marton needed to stay off the grid. Pedro had given him the key to the Czartoryski family's riverboat moored on the south end of the Pegnitz River. The boat was docked permanently, with easy access to the Rhein-Main-Donau-Kanal. The canal, one hundred six miles long, connected the Main and Danube Rivers and provided navigation from the North Sea and the Atlantic Ocean to the Black Sea.

The riverboat was actually a small yacht. He wasn't going to cruise in it—just spend a few nights. He needed privacy, and for that, it was perfect.

After unpacking his bag, he pulled out of a small case a red wig, a sport coat, dark-framed glasses, and a cap that he could pull down to his nose. He changed from his boots to tennis shoes and put together the pieces of a walking stick. Satisfied with his cover, he picked up the walking stick and left the riverboat.

His watch told him that getting to the tavern at the prearranged time would be tight. Fortunately, he was able to catch a taxi and make the appointment.

The man from the BfV, Simon Bell, would not be pleased if he were late.

CHAPTER THIRTEEN

The German Government

BfV—The Federal Office for the Protection of the Constitution

Simon Bell was sitting in a back booth, eating a sausage and drinking a beer. Despite Marton's disguise, he waved at him. "Have a beer."

Marton laughed. "*Ja*, the most famous foods in Germany: the Nuremberg sausage and a tankard of *Landbier*."

"I forget you have traveled over our country almost as if you were employed by the BfV," said Simon. "Oh, excuse me, you are one of our employees. You have been protecting our country from antidemocratic forces and from neo-Nazis."

Marton shook his head. "I will either have a good pension or be dead. I am trying to keep the neo-Nazi right-wingers under control. Now, tell me what I need to know."

"You go first with what you have found out," said Simon.

Marton laughed. "I do not have much more than I did at our last meeting. Like I told you in Vilnius, I killed the monk."

Simon nodded and said, "You are in the clear. Our sources in Vilnius tell us that one of the Grey Eagles killed him. They were afraid he would talk."

"What?" asked Marton, glad to be off the hook for the killing. "Did the old guy really know where the rest of the gold was?"

Simon shrugged. "He knew gold was in the Czartoryski mansion. What else he knew, who can say."

They sipped their beer and munched on the sausages, dipping them in hot mustard.

Simon brought him up to speed. "We know the group is going to do something. The chatter from the Grey Eagles is on the reemergence of the Fourth Reich. This information makes sense because almost everyone who lived during the Third Reich is dead. A local chapter will hold a march tomorrow. More marches are scheduled, and the participants will get rough. Injuries to police and marchers will be unavoidable."

Marton realized that he had just heard about the march from Pedro that morning. Simon, though, was on a roll.

"Seventy-five years have passed since the Third Reich was destroyed in World War II. Though bombed and defeated, the movement never died. Neo-Nazis are today plotting to resurrect a new Reich."

Both men knew that the gold was more important now than ever. No movement existed on ideas alone. Money was required for a new Reich.

"Simon, do your men carry guns? This march could get nasty."

"No guns, Marton. They do not carry weapons, cannot arrest people, and have no police authority because in the past, the police abused their power. I agree that they could use guns for protection against the Grey Eagles, who do carry weapons."

"The Grey Eagles will never stop until they find the lost gold bullion," said Marton.

Simon agreed. "When they find the gold is when the trouble will begin. How close are you to finding the gold?"

"I am doing my best to locate it. So far, neither the Grey Eagles nor international groups like the one in Paraguay know where it is."

"Keep looking, Marton, because they are looking. I know Pedro is your friend, but do not be fooled. His father and his brother run the Grey Eagles here in Nuremberg."

Marton knew that Simon was right. Nothing had changed for a generation. Whoever controlled Nuremberg controlled Germany.

CHAPTER FOURTEEN

The Grey Eagles

Bazyli Czartoryski's new estate in Nuremberg was on the east side of the city. The location had been chosen carefully. The property was on a residential street with twenty-four-hour bus service, ideal for visitors who did not own a car. His two sons, Pedro and Uwe, lived there with a handful of domestic servants. The old man still preferred the family estate outside Vienna.

Some might have thought it strange that Polish nobility had chosen Nuremberg for their mattress factory. Bazyli corrected that impression by making sure that the Nuremberg business leaders knew that he needed competent workers. Nuremburg was known for having a large labor pool. He added that his mother's family was from Hamburg, making it seem like he was really German. No one could check if it was true. Sometimes, the destruction of records in World War II was useful. He lived in Vienna, said it was for taxes, and no one questioned him.

At least once a week, a half dozen or so men—young and middle-aged—took the bus out to the Czartoryski home. Dressed casually, they looked as though they were going to a meeting of the local soccer team. They drank beer, smoked Moroccan cigars, and pledged allegiance to the Grey Eagles. Tonight was different. They were planning a march through the city.

Bazyli passed around a bottle of a premium German brandy. He stood up, looking shorter than his six-foot frame because he was almost as wide. His bald head, always glowing, was a beacon in the meeting room. When he laughed, he twirled his black-and-gray moustache.

He held up his crystal glass. "To the march."

The men downed their shots. One man spoke up. "We need to carry weapons. *Ja*, the law says we cannot carry arms, but the police, even without pistols, can be rough."

Uwe agreed, saying they needed weapons. "The police are protected in all that riot gear."

"*Nein, nein*," said Bazyli. "We can't violate the law."

"The laws will kill us," protested Uwe. He looked like his father, only thinner and physically fit. "We need to show our supporters we are engaged. The television cameras will be rolling. I have seen to that. Our march will be a recruiting tool, as you have often said."

His father laughed. "Yes, that is why we march." He passed another bottle of brandy around the room. "This time, keep the march peaceful. Our day will come. We are not ready. Our men are still getting in place across Germany."

They toasted, and as they went to leave, Uwe handed each one an envelope. As usual, the envelope contained four thousand euros. One man paused and quietly explained that two of his family members were ill. He needed more funds to care for them. Bazyli hugged him and stuffed two more envelopes in his coat pocket. The men left quickly to catch the city bus.

Uwe looked at his father. "We have to start attacking the police." He could tell his father was distracted.

"Uwe, you must understand weapons are nothing. It is all about the money. And the purse is almost empty. How long can we continue to subsidize our members' needs, legitimate as they are? We must find more gold."

"Pedro met with Marton, who is looking for it. Father, you have said for some time that we need to execute our own search."

Bazyli nodded. "Without the gold, we can kiss the Fourth Reich goodbye."

Uwe understood the need for gold but knew his father did not want to be aggressive and alienate people who might join their cause. Now was the time, in Uwe's mind, for the Grey Eagles to be aggressive. The march tomorrow would show the German people there was support for the right-wing political movements.

• • •

To Marton, the view of the city from the documents center was almost enough to make him forget why he was there. Once, the city had been the center of the Holy Roman Empire. Today, it was one of Germany's industrial centers, as it had been before and during World War II.

To the north, the city was dominated by Kaiserburg, the castle built in the twelfth century to house the treasures of the Holy Roman Empire. To the south were the parade grounds and the stadium seen in Nazi propaganda films. Some of the grounds had been destroyed during the war, but Marton could see that the size and scope were immense.

He pulled himself away from the view and entered the administration building, following signs to the learning center. The clerk was efficient and gave Marton his own computer and workspace.

"Are all of the historic files on the computer?" Marton wanted to be sure that he was looking at all the documents from the past.

"Yes," said the clerk, and she returned to her desk.

Marton thought about the words to use for his search. The obvious word was *Gold*, which was the same in both English and German. Only, he knew the Germans had more names: *Golden*, *Geld*, *Goldfarbe*, and *Goldton*.

He stared at the screen, looking at the matches. *Gold* had over two million hits. *Gold bullion* would narrow the search, or *gold bullion transferred*. That combination did, indeed, further narrow the search. Then, he remembered *Raubgold*, the word used for the stolen Nazi gold. He entered the search term, and within a few seconds, the computer produced a hundred eighty references. No way could he review all of them.

He thought for a moment. During the war, bullion was shipped out of Germany. One destination he knew was Paraguay. The Germans in that country had been living off the gold for decades. Now, they—and other Germans scattered around the world—needed more money, more gold, if they were going to build the Fourth Reich.

He forced himself to forget for a moment that even his friend Pedro thought he was on the side of the Grey Eagles. To find the gold, he had to think like one of the Grey Eagles.

Without money, the Grey Eagles would collapse. Without funds, neo-Nazi members would have to work. With less time spent plotting the return of the Reich, countries would be able to track the members and break up the cells. Goodbye to forming the Fourth Reich.

I will be here for days, he thought, *but I am stupid. All I need is transfers in 1945, the last year of the war.*

Marton knew that it sounded simple, but it was not. He typed in a new search for *1945*. He had to hurry. The holiday markets opened before noon, and he didn't want to miss any of the march.

CHAPTER FIFTEEN

March of the Grey Eagles

Amy looked over the Hauptmarkt, a bustling square in the center of Nuremberg. Every day, it was filled with kiosks for shopping, and now, there were additional kiosks for the goods for the famous *Christkindlesmarkt.*

She was glad Sonora had insisted on the trip to Nuremberg. Thoren's aunt was ill. Since her signature was needed to access the safe-deposit box, they would have to wait for her health to improve. The trip to see the Christmas markets was the perfect outing. Besides, Sonora thought they needed a break from all the fuss about gold. The Christmas markets were unique, and the search for gold could wait.

Nuremberg had the largest holiday market in Germany, if not in Europe. Wandering around the kiosks was something she enjoyed doing as Christmastime approached. Everything seemed to be for sale, from handmade crafts and clothes to Christmas decorations and food. The smell of the food was tantalizing, and tasting samples was always a priority.

What to buy was her problem. There were cakes, breads, puddings, and cookies, all elaborately decorated. In the end, she chose the gingerbread Christmas cake, as much for herself as for Sonora. It was her aunt's favorite.

"I knew you'd buy the cake, so I didn't."

Amy turned around to see Ace working his way between the stalls. She could see that Middle Eastern food had agreed with him. He was even fatter than when he had left for the conference. Fortunately, he was six feet four and carried the weight well. His height was a Prowers trait, but otherwise, her cousin looked like his mother: square head and blond-gray hair.

As tall as he was, all she could see were the bundles in his hands and the Christmas bags he was carrying. For a moment, she thought he had bought the entire market—at least the food products.

"Look at these hams. They're smoked, so we can take them back to Berlin without a problem."

"Great," replied Amy. She was glad they had rooms at the hotel where they could stay overnight; otherwise, they'd be carrying their purchases all day long.

Ace had plans for the evening. "Amy, let's leave the food items in our hotel rooms and get an early start on dinner. The

Bratwursthäusle is said to have the best food in the city and has a view of the Hauptmarkt. We have a lot to discuss."

Amy agreed and found herself enjoying the atmosphere as she followed him down the crowded street. An occasional snow shower added to the ambience of the season. She was sure of only one thing; her cousin had a good reason for the early dinner, and it was not to start eating and drinking.

The evening, she thought, *is going to be interesting.*

Looking at the other shoppers, she wondered if they had a relative who made every event an intrigue.

The table Ace had reserved had a view of the market and the street. Amy couldn't see why the view was so important but didn't have to wait long to find out.

"A neo-Nazi march is scheduled for late afternoon, just in time for tonight's news. I wanted to see it but not to be in the middle of it. Sonora never would have shipped us off if she'd known about the march."

"It will be an event," said Amy. "In the past, I wasn't interested in neo-Nazis or right-wing groups. But after I found Vince's journal and map, I realized that the Nazis are among us. Now, they're targeting refugees. That bothers me. Tell me, where are you getting information about these groups? I thought they were a secret society, a rogue movement for dissatisfied Germans."

Ace said she was right on all counts. "During my years in the military, I had a good friend who was German. We undertook a number of missions, jointly with the German government. Today, Simon Bell is a deputy in their domestic intelligence agency. The official title is terrible: the Federal Office for the Protection of the Constitution. It's referred to as the BfV. The organization is paranoid about the refugees and about the neo-Nazis."

He paused and looked around the room. "Sonora and her Committee have an interest in many groups. Some of the most influential men in the world are on the Committee. Our grandfather, when he founded it, was not into the masses. It was for the elites. Sonora has kept his model but included several members our grandfather would never have approved. I'm glad you're going to join us."

Without making any promises, Amy told Ace she intended to be at the future meetings. "I like them online."

Ace agreed. Security was easy online.

Their conversation was interrupted by the arrival of the waiter with menus. The restaurant was busy, so they made a quick decision to order *Rostbratwürste*, the famous bratwurst flame grilled on a beechwood grill. With the waiter's help, they selected the local red beer. Ace ordered two of everything.

According to the waiter, the beer was brewed in copper kettles using hops naturally grown and fermented in wooden fermenting vats. He motioned to another waiter, who immediately set two large drafts of beer on the table.

Before they could take a sip, Ace asked to change tables. The waiter looked surprised but said they had an empty table back in the bar. Amy didn't question his request—just waited for him to explain.

"I think the table I reserved may have been bugged. The Germans are very high-tech and sensitive to what they perceive as infringements on their liberties. The truth is they are better at spying than our American government."

"Ace, I know you thought Sonora's house was bugged."

"Yes, and that they didn't find anything convinces me even more that it's still bugged."

Amy thought the same thing. Her aunt's car had been bugged, so why not the house?

Ace drained his beers, both of them, and ordered red wine, knowing Amy preferred red.

"Amy, I know you think I'm being paranoid, but any business when neo-Nazis are around is dangerous."

He went on to tell her about how the head of the BfV had recently resigned because of a cover-up of a neo-Nazi cell that had killed over twenty people of Turkish descent who were German citizens. The German police found that the cell had operated for over a decade—with help from office staff from the BfV. That office destroyed records that might have exposed those who had collaborated with the neo-Nazi group.

"But Amy, we have to remember, this investigation is dangerous. No one in the German government seems to know what was in the files that were destroyed. Such ambiguity means that someone's lying. When we're back in Berlin, I'll look at the map and try to figure out where the gold might be."

Amy looked around the busy restaurant. A three-piece band was playing. She thought Ace had picked a great place to have a confidential conversation. Her cousin was drinking, and it was a good time to get him to talk. She often had a hard time getting a word in edgewise when he was on his computer.

"The Abbot told me Marton's a neo-Nazi." She said it as if she was reading the front page of the *London Times*.

Ace didn't even bother to look around the room before he spoke. The noise from other tables, the congestion of people coming in and leaving the restaurant, was a perfect cover.

"Amy, the Abbot is a Nazi. Look at the facts. How did he manage to maintain St. Benedict's behind the Berlin Wall? He survived for decades in East Germany. He's Stasi. Marton works for the BfV but is inside the neo-Nazi groups. I don't have to tell you not to repeat that. Trust me, he's one of us."

Amy asked if Sonora knew. Ace nodded. "But she believes in keeping in contact with the Abbot, who seems to know everyone in Berlin. You know that old adage, 'Keep your enemies closer.'"

While they talked, noise from the street drowned out the band. Amy got up and looked outside. What had been a busy street was now a mob scene. The Grey Eagles were marching ten abreast, filling the street.

"The police are not going to like this," said Ace, who motioned to the waiter for another lager.

Amy was thinking of America. "It's a good thing no one carries a gun."

"But they do," said Ace. "They just don't use them."

The words were hardly out of his mouth when they heard the sound of gunfire. Amy's natural reaction was to look out the window, but she knew that was dangerous.

"Do we hide under the table?" To Amy, her question sounded absurd but logical.

"No, just don't look out the window," said Ace.

As he spoke, more shots erupted. Two couples at a table behind them got up and left, their plates still full of food. Ace motioned to the waiter and asked what was going on.

"So sorry for the noise. These marches often take place, and the police do nothing. They claim there are not enough police officers because they are dealing with refugee problems, not marches."

Amy asked if the refugee camps were near this area or outside the city.

"They are outside the city, but the refugees do not stay in the camps," said the waiter. "The Brown Shirts do not go to the camps. The refugees are tough."

He was interrupted by a volley of shots, and the manager announced that everyone was to move away from the windows and into the interior bar. The waiter said that he would serve their food in the bar. Amy and Ace did not have to be asked twice.

As they moved to the bar, the noise from the street, shouting and the banging of drums, followed them. The bar was crowded, with most of the customers on their cell phones, trying to find out what was happening. Ace turned his on.

"How do they get the news so soon?" He answered his own question. "Easy, the cell phone camera."

She heard more muffled gunfire.

"Sounds like the street is really getting shot up. The news feed is behind."

She looked over Ace's shoulder at the pictures on his phone. The street looked like a war zone. Helmeted police were coming up the street, apparently to clear it. The screen went blank as the waiter brought their wine.

"This is the refugee problem," said the waiter. "Too many of them, and they do not share our history or our values. The population is aging, and we need refugees to do the work. The Brown Shirts hate them. Wine?"

Ace declined the offer and said, "Maybe it's a mistake, but I'm going out on the street, just for a few minutes."

Amy looked at the waiter and nodded for him to pour her some wine. "It's my cousin's action complex. He can't miss watching bullets fly." She paused as they heard more gunfire. "Ace, going out there is crazy."

Ace was already getting up. "I'll stay on the porch."

Amy laughed at his parting words. She knew him and also knew that nothing could keep him from the street. She looked at her glass of wine. Drinking was all she could do at a time like this.

Gunfire erupted in the street again. She took a big sip of wine. This was Ace's world. She had to hope he'd be safe.

• • •

Ace looked down at the chaos on the street and in the market. Stalls were overturned, and debris was scattered everywhere. Bodies were lying in the street—shoppers, he presumed, and several bodies clad in brown shirts. Nobody was going to be pleased with this carnage. He understood why the press had stopped publishing videos. They were graphic, and reporters could be sued.

The first responders were hovering around all the bodies, except four that were covered with gray blankets. The speed with which they had arrived told him that they knew the march was coming and were prepared.

Most of the neo-Nazis had left the scene by slipping away down the side streets. Ace knew they carried other shirts or jackets to cover their brown shirts, making it easier to simply retreat into the local crowd. He knew that within the hour, the street would be clear. The Germans would never tolerate a mess.

As he headed down the stairs, he heard a shout. In front of him, on a sheet, was another body wearing a brown shirt. None of this was new to him. He watched the police search the body for identification. When they found it, they stood up and moved to the side to call in the name on the phone. They didn't cover the face.

Ace looked at the body—he didn't know the man—and then hurried back to the hotel restaurant. He had seen enough. He had to get back to Amy in the restaurant before the police started questioning spectators.

Amy wasn't interested in the neo-Nazi movement. She was involved only because she believed that some of them might help her find the gold. He had to make her understand the danger and the need to protect herself.

To interpret the journal and the map, she needed help. She had known Vince better than anyone and ought to be able to understand the clues he had left so many years ago.

He saw the look of relief on her face as he entered the restaurant. "Amy, I'll skip telling you about the carnage on the street because we have to get back to Berlin. Vince left clues in the journal and with the map. We have to find them. The rest of this is just killing time—time we might not have."

She looked up from her wine glass. "Let's go back now. Trains run to Berlin all night. We've seen the market, bought gifts, so it's time to go."

"Couldn't agree more," said Ace. "Let me finish this wine."

Amy laughed. "I'm sure they'll serve plenty of liquor on the train."

• • •

Marton had been moving along the edge of the street with the Brown Shirts. He couldn't dodge the cluster of first responders ahead of him. They had been working on one of the injured people.

He heard the first responder say that there was nothing more they could do. As he tried to walk by, he found himself looking at the dead man. It was Uwe Czartoryski.

Oh, shit! was his first thought.

He wasn't upset over Uwe dying. The guy was a hothead and seemed destined for an early death. Rather, his concern was how the Czartoryski family would take the death. He knew Bazyli by reputation and realized that he might take his time, but eventually, someone would pay for his son's death.

CHAPTER SIXTEEN

Vince's Findings

Amy looked out at Unter den Linden as soft, fluffy snowflakes touched the ground. She was glad to be back in Berlin.

Everyone, including Sonora, agreed that someone had bugged her house and her cars. No one was certain that they had found all the bugs. Compared to the house, the hotel seemed like a safe haven.

For her peace of mind, she was the only one who had the combination to the safe in the hotel room.

Why she felt she had to have the map, she didn't know. Ace had gone to get a copy from Sonora.

Maybe she should call the Abbot to have another lunch. Until they translated the journal or understood the map, all possible connections to the past needed to be kept alive. No telling what he might have to say or what he knew about the Grey Eagles. Living behind the wall in East Germany all those years had to give him some perspective.

The good news was that the map and the journal were in the safe in Sonora's home, and no one but Sonora knew the combination. Her aunt's house was full of security personnel searching for bugs, so she was not staying at her house. No one would think that she would keep something so valuable in the hotel apartment. Vince always said being obvious was the best security. She hoped so.

Thank God Sonora had insisted on making a copy of the map and the journal. The original ones were locked in the family's safe-deposit box at a German bank. Which bank, Sonora would never say.

"Security is in telling no one," she often said. So, now, there were three safes: the bank, the hotel, and Sonora's house.

She shook her head, tired of thinking about all the safes, then found herself looking over the street to see if anyone was watching the hotel. The patio of the coffee shop across the street was closed, but its windows looked out on the empty boulevard as the snow continued to fall.

There was a knock on the door. It was Ace.

"This better tell us something," Amy said as Ace entered the apartment, carrying a small, cheap, inconspicuous knapsack.

He patted the knapsack. "Let's take a look at the map." He pulled a large magnifying glass out of a desk drawer and said, "Vince may have highlighted some notes we missed."

After nearly an hour of searching with the magnifying glass, they found nothing. Amy was frustrated. "Should Marton look at the map? Maybe I'm overly cautious, but Vince kept it a secret for a reason."

Ace agreed. "I'll call Sonora. She should be able to get Marton to come to the hotel today."

While he called, Amy took another look at the map. Something on it had to have meaning. Otherwise, Vince would never have kept it so secure and hidden, not showing anyone its contents.

Why was it important to the London bankers who died in the plane crash so many years ago? she wondered.

The gold could be transported north or south. South was Austria and southern Germany, the area where gold hunters and neo-Nazis thought the gold had been used to fund a new Reich. The gold had been hidden in the mountains, and much of that gold had been found after World War II by the American military.

The question was, why would the Nazis hide gold in southern Germany and risk transporting it over the mountains and through hundreds of small villages? Those villages had eyes and ears. Again, she found herself thinking that the gold had to go north.

"Ace, listen to this. The gold can't get to South America without going by ship, submarine, whatever. So, take the gold north; it's risky, but in the end, the gold gets out of Europe faster than going overland through Spain or Portugal. The risk of going north is that the ship carrying the gold would have to travel the length of the Atlantic Ocean. On the plus side, no one has been looking for Nazi gold transported down the middle of the North Atlantic."

She paused for a moment. "Norway is farther north. From a port up there, water routes going west would simply go out to the center of the North Atlantic and head south. No nation can patrol the entire Atlantic. Something to think about."

Ace agreed and said he was ready for lunch. Amy suggested they eat at the restaurant across from the hotel. "It's popular with the Grey Eagles. Who knows who we could meet? I'll lock up the map and the journal."

He agreed. Without asking, Amy knew that it was very likely that Ace had at least two guns tucked away on his person or in the knapsack he always carried, just in case of an emergency.

Berlin's skies were cloudy in the late fall, but typically, little snow fell. Today, it was falling furiously as they crossed Unter der Linden to the café. According to the waitress, the restaurant served over forty German beers. They ordered a local beer and ham and cheese sandwiches, with Ace ordering two of each.

"At this rate, my cholesterol will be out-of-sight," he said.

Both cousins were very healthy, considering they ate vegetables only accidentally or when included with a meal.

Amy looked around the room, as if she expected to see someone she knew. She noticed that Ace had put the knapsack under his chair. As big as he was, it would take a couple of men to get to it.

"You're going to recognize the Grey Eagles," said Amy. "They all have shaved heads and short beards."

At that, Ace had to laugh. He stopped and engaged the waitress, whose English was quite good. "I hear this is a meeting place for the Grey Eagles."

The waitress, a well-proportioned blonde in her late thirties, didn't deny it. "Call me Marta," she said. "Why you want to know? They are bad people."

"*Ja*," said Ace, "but they are in here all the time. They watch the hotel."

"So, why do you want to know?"

Ace went into an explanation that seemed to say that he might want to join the group. Instead of being insulted, the waitress said that she could introduce him to one of the leaders.

"He is in here all the time. Only not today."

Ace said he would be back and proceeded to dive into the sandwiches, which Amy admitted were delicious.

"Another day in paradise," said Ace.

Amy looked out at the snow pelting the ground but not staying. "I feel like I've been on vacation, but you know we've got to get the journal translated."

"Yep. Old Latin. Whoever thought that up must have been a monk."

She agreed. "The monks seem to be following us everywhere."

"What about the monks at the Gračanica Monastery?" asked Ace.

He knew that was where they had found the Shroud of Turin several years ago. The Shroud, a piece of linen, had for centuries been believed to be the burial cloth of Jesus Christ.

"The Abbot died; he was nearly a hundred. Medak could help. I know he speaks German—and obviously Latin. He's a good guy, but I hate to involve him in this gold business."

She paused for a moment. "Order more beer and hang out to see if any neo-Nazis arrive. While you wait, I'll visit the Abbot. The monastery's only a mile from here. I called him, and he said to stop by anytime. Visiting him will please Sonora." She added that she had already texted the Abbot.

Ace didn't have to be told twice and motioned to the waitress for another beer. "Hurry back," he said as she left.

• • •

Amy was on the east side of Berlin, so far to the east she felt like she was in Poland. Her GPS finally indicated a turn off the main road. Suddenly, she was in a maze of old German houses, and she was thankful for the GPS. Crossing a bridge, she noticed that the landscape opened up, and she saw St. Benedict's Monastery along the river. Behind it were what looked like orchards, likely where the hops were grown. She knew the monastery made money from producing beer. The practice had long been a way for religious orders to make money.

The monastery had a small parking lot, and as she pulled in, she saw the tall, blond Abbot waiting at the main door to greet her.

"Amy, come in out of the snow. Rarely does it snow in Berlin, and never when it is convenient. I am pleased to see you again."

The gate closed softly behind them. Amy found herself looking at a building in the center of the monastery with a beer parlor attached to one side.

"We only serve beer for religious festivals. In southern Germany, some monasteries produce several hundred thousand gallons of beer, and one or two over a million gallons. Here, we are only a small producer and sell almost nothing commercially. Would you like to see the vats?"

"Yes, very much," said Amy, following the Abbot into the center building.

Inside, she saw that crucifixes hung on the walls behind the vats. The Abbot said the monastery had been making beer since the Middle Ages. Most of the production was done in the south in Bavarian monasteries that had been producing beer for over four hundred years. He said beer was food in the days of old was safer to drink than water.

"Today, most German monasteries have been taken over by private brewers. The monasteries developed brewing procedures that made German beer great. After World War II, monasteries modernized. We continued to pump beer out for our customers until we no longer needed the income. Today, we produce enough for religious holidays. Shall we sit in the parlor and have a glass? We keep a supply for occasions like this."

The Abbot must have read Amy's mind. She sipped her beer. It was smooth yet full bodied—not bitter.

The Abbot paused, not wanting to overstate his case. He was not a believer in the Reich. The new group of right-wingers, since they couldn't be called Nazis in Germany, had no idea of his politics. His background made him one of them. The real irony was that they asked no questions, just assumed he was one of them. One day, he would have to make a decision about whose side he was on. He and Bazyli had discussed forming their own party. Who knew what lay ahead in German politics?

"You know I am here with the support of your family."

Looking around, Amy wondered where the money had gone. The church and monastery house needed paint and some roof repairs.

The Abbot poured another round of beer. Marton had told him Amy was looking for the gold. He should give her something to use. He had trusted Frederic with the gold when it was moved out of Berlin. He thought with Frederic's connections to the investment banking world, the gold would be safe. That was a mistake. Now, he was working both sides and trusting no one.

One day, Frederic might return. If he did, then he would have his own team of right-wingers take care of him. Until then, he had to listen to all the carping, particularly from Czartoryski, about where the gold was.

"Amy, after the war, the gold—I cannot say how much—was hidden under the vats in this brewery. It was stored here for decades before Frederic took it to Vilnius about the time Vince died. Then, Frederic disappeared. I believe he stashed the gold somewhere between Berlin and the Baltic. My sources have been trying to find him, without any luck."

He hadn't told her the whole truth. Frederic had moved the gold from Vilnius to his wife's house in Husum, where it stayed for years. Then, about five years ago, he moved it back to this monastery. They stored the trucks overnight, which was how he had gotten the small amount of bullion that Bazyli was due. They left the next day for Switzerland and for Count Lliessle's bank. Then, Frederic disappeared in South Africa. Facts were what he lacked. No need to bother Amy with suppositions. Working in East Germany for decades, he had learned to stick to the facts.

Amy composed herself and asked, "How much gold was Frederic moving over northern Europe?"

The Abbot wasn't going to get into a calculation that would never be accurate. Transporting gold was iffy. A bar or two would go missing at every exchange. What he said to Amy was that the gold was measured in bullion and that the value depended on the price of gold at any point in time. In truth, he just saw the wooden crates and had no idea how much gold was in them. He threw out a figure to her: over a billion.

After another beer, Amy thanked the Abbot and left for the hotel. All she could think about were his words: *over a billion*. So many people knew about the gold.

The Abbot watched her drive away. He was certain she would go north to find the gold. He was pleased. If she was good at following clues, and he thought she was, then she would find out if there was any gold left in Husum. He never was sure that Frederic had brought all of it out.

For now, he would wait and see. All he knew for sure was that during his last trip, Frederic had taken the gold from the monastery to Switzerland. The route from Husum, with the stop at the monastery, didn't make much sense unless Frederic took some of the gold for himself. He had no proof, but then, gold drove men to do strange things.

CHAPTER SEVENTEEN

Vienna

For the Abbot, it was business as usual at the monastery, until he took a call from Bazyli. The old man's first sentence said it all: "My son Uwe is dead. They killed him."

The Abbot was sympathetic. "Bazyli, I saw the news reports on the march, but I did not know it was Uwe who died." He paused, waiting for the old man to tell him why he was calling.

"I have been neutral to your cause—but not anymore. Find the gold, and I will get it to a country in South America for you. My factories have contracts with shipping companies. You are right. Now is the time for us to form our own movement."

The Abbot had waited a long time for Bazyli to support another movement they would create. He never thought much of

Uwe, having seen him in meetings. Now, his death was proving to be profitable. The Abbot knew vengeance was all Bazyli could think about.

"What can I do now?" asked Bazyli.

"Nothing, my friend. Sit tight. There are new ideas on where the gold could be, and I will follow up on them."

"Stay in touch."

Bazyli hung up.

The Abbot was pleased. Not so much that Uwe, who was usually drunk and a hothead, was dead but that Bazyli's other son, Pedro, was smart. His brother's death would make him the leader of the new group that he and Bazyli would form.

He looked at the logs crackling in the fireplace.

What is my plan?

The gold was hidden somewhere in Germany. The records of gold transfers during the war from London and those of Swiss banks proved that.

Like everyone else, the Abbot believed that the journal had been destroyed when Vince was killed. Vince wouldn't have taken it to Pakistan with him; he would have left it somewhere. Where? Had to be Berlin. Amy Prowers was now in Berlin. Did she have Vince's journal? Did she have the map? Misha was sure she had one.

I need to contact Marton. And I will stay close to Sonora until I find out what Amy and Ace are up to.

CHAPTER EIGHTEEN

In Berlin at the Restaurant

Ace was eating and drinking in the restaurant across from the hotel. Amy, back from seeing the Abbot, was looking at the menu after talking to Sonora on the phone.

"Sonora says that Marton may be the only one who can translate this journal. He helped Vince with translations, meanings of specific words. She also didn't think Vince showed anyone the map since he was so secretive about what he was doing. I agree with her. She also talked to Marton, who's at the museum. She asked him to meet us here, at the restaurant. The Kempinski is only a few minutes away from the museum."

Amy laughed and looked up at Ace. "She's pleased that I met the Abbot. I don't know why. He raised questions, but I did get to see the brewery operation at the monastery. Is this a safe place to talk to Marton?"

"Yes." Ace sounded very sure. "Let me show you the latest toy." He took out a device that resembled a cell phone. "See the man at the table by the window?" They both looked at the device, which showed a picture of a cell phone. "Not a threat," said Ace, "and no one else has any electronics on."

"Unlike the hotel," interjected Amy.

"Right."

Ace went on to say that every room at the Kempinski could be bugged. "It's an old hotel, but renovations have been extensive. We have to watch ourselves."

"I can see why my apartment would be a target, but you're in the other wing."

"Just easier to bug," said Ace. He ordered more beer—and one for Marton, who would be arriving any minute.

"Skip me," said Amy. "I had enough beer with the Abbot."

Ace sipped his beer and pulled out a copy of the journal, which was really a small spiral notebook with a leather cover. He flipped through it. Only about ten pages were filled. He handed it to Amy.

She knew this was a copy and was glad the real one was locked up. Looking at the words, she saw that the language resembled German. Problem was, many of the words were archaic, making it almost another language. She hoped Marton could translate it.

The margins had a few notes. How typical that was of Vince. He always used the margins. Often, what he put there was important. He thought of it as his private code.

Turning the book sidewise to read the margins, she saw words that made no sense. Two names were listed: Ludwig and Gottfried. No last names. To her, that seemed odd. Ace interrupted her as Marton entered the restaurant.

"You got here fast."

"*Ja*, thanks for the beer." He sat down and sipped it as Amy handed him the journal.

"It's what Vince found and is now his legacy. It's misdirection from his grave. I just noticed two names. Why would he put them in the margins?"

Marton shrugged and opened the journal. He read quickly, flipping the pages. "Both of you have read this?"

"I get the drift, but the ancient words are foreign to me," said Ace.

"Then you know," said Marton, "it is a story, a tale of spirits hiding in a castle and in the lakes that surround it. The islands in northern Germany, Sylt and Frisian Islands, are mentioned."

Ace looked at Amy. "Again, going north comes up."

"The tale is what we call an illusion, using symbols to tell a story," said Marton.

Ace and Amy looked at each other. Amy spoke first. "How like Vince to be into smoke and mirrors. So, we're looking for a castle on the north German or Danish coast. We need a map." She reached into her knapsack and pulled one out. It was one of the maps her father kept in the desk in the apartment at the Kempinski. Silently, she thanked him.

Marton pointed north of Berlin to the area south of the Danish border. "Husum is a jumping-off point to the northeast coast and those islands. I once visited Sylt Island. The Frisian Islands are in shallow grounds, actually mudflats. Big ships or submarines cannot get to the coast." The two cousins watched Marton's finger as it traced the route to Husum.

Ace chugged his beer and motioned to the waitress for another round before speaking. "Small boats can shuttle people across the mudflats out to the submarines or larger ships. Just because they can't land, doesn't mean they could use it as a jumping-off point. I keep looking farther north toward Norway. And like I said, ships from that country can immediately be in the North Atlantic and then head south to South America. The size of the Atlantic Ocean will protect them."

"The real question," said Amy, "is if the gold got to South America."

They were silent. All the talk was about the gold going to South America, but no one had any proof.

Marton had heard enough. He stood up and excused himself, saying that he had to get back to work. "If you need any more help, let me know. I am pleased to assist."

"Appreciate your help, Marton."

Marton grinned. "It is exciting. This is a real find."

"That it is," said Amy. Although, she really thought finding the gold would be the real find.

Amy asked the waitress for a cup of coffee and added an order of bratwurst. She felt she was going to need it.

Ace was studying the journal. He was looking at Vince's notes on the back cover. They were almost illegible. He barely made out two names, Lewis Chadwick and Jeffery March, with the words "Bank of England."

"Amy, what are the German names for Lewis and for Jeffery?"

She looked up from her computer search. "How about Ludwig and Gottfried? Both names were listed in the margins in the journal."

"Do Bank of England officials have to be English? I mean, the bank had major holdings in Switzerland," said Ace.

Amy didn't know but thought they could be another nationality. She knew what Ace was thinking: that the names might be a key to where the gold was hidden.

"Ace, we may be grasping at straws, but the names could be important. If we use the computer at Sonora's, we can get a printout. It will be safer than using the printer at the hotel."

"You're right, and that's why I'm going to stay here and drink. And chat with Marta. I want to impress upon her that I am also a right-winger. Can't hurt if she knows the Grey Eagles. Tell Sonora I'm looking at a connection."

"Okay," said Amy.

• • •

Marton knew it was dangerous going to St. Benedict's Monastery, but he could get in a back way that was little known, even to the locals. The Abbot's profile wasn't as anonymous as he thought. It was very likely that the BfV had the main door under surveillance.

Because the monastery had been in East Germany for decades, the Abbot had to know many secrets. Marton suspected that the Abbot had more secrets than the current German secu-rity services on German government employees.

The Abbot was surprised to see him. More than one visitor a day was unusual.

"You left the gate unlocked. It is not safe," said Marton.

The Abbot was patronizing. "We are protected." Even as he said it, the Abbot wondered how much protection the monastery really had.

The Abbot asked, "What is the Prowers family trying to find? Amy did not seem to know."

Marton shrugged. "Abbot, they are not stupid."

The Abbot thought for a moment. "Keep me informed if they come up with anything. You know Bazyli?"

Marton paused, wanting to appear ignorant. "The Russian living outside Vienna?"

"Yes. Though everyone thinks he is Polish, he professes to be German. He always thought Amy's husband Vince figured out where the gold was hidden."

Marton shook his head. "I worked with Vince. It was years ago. All he found was an Old Latin narrative that was a journal. Nothing else."

The Abbot shook his head. "Bazyli always believed Vince found something."

Marton left thinking the Abbot trusted him, yet something struck him as odd about what was in Vince's journal. He just couldn't put his finger on it. If Vince found the gold, then he would have said so.

• • •

Marton was sure no one had followed him to the monastery. Leaving it was something else.

This place is under surveillance, he thought.

A small, nondescript sedan, he was certain, was following him. The car he was driving was another nondescript sedan, but under the hood was a special engine. He down shifted and lost the other sedan at the roundabout.

He pulled over on a side street and waited until the sedan had cleared the roundabout. Slowly, he pulled out, and through back streets, he worked his way to the address for the safe house Simon Bell had given him.

Once inside the safe house, he poured himself a double vodka. He realized that he needed to be careful. There was a lot at stake—a billion or so in gold, to be precise.

• • •

Amy turned in to Sonora's entry gate and saw the circular drive-way filled with cars. The house lights were all on, and it looked like her aunt was hosting a party.

"I've ordered a complete security review," her aunt announced. She understood that Amy needed to do some research on the computer. As for Ace, she hoped he wouldn't get too drunk at the café.

Amy headed to the library and then saw Thoren, who waved her over. "I cannot leave, Miss Amy." He looked around. "I am keeping an eye on the security guy who is searching for bugs. Sonora said she told you that my mother was ill and that we still have not gotten to the bank. Now, she is feeling better and ready to go to the bank. Tomorrow, we will be at the bank to open the deposit box. Can you come with us?"

Amy said she'd be pleased to go to the bank with them.

"Now, Thoren, I may need your help on this computer." She pointed to the library, explaining that she needed to use Sonora's computer and printer. "It has a bigger screen, so you can also see all of the searches."

Turning the computer on, Amy decided to do a search and typed in *castles*. She paused.

What was the name of that province north of Berlin? Mecklenburg?

She typed it in. A list of castles came up.

She realized that this was not going to work.

What was the name of the program Ace always used?

She got out her phone and texted him at the café. He replied immediately: "What you're doing must be more productive than reading the journal. Look up asset mapping."

She typed in *asset mapping*, and the program came up. Filling out the spaces was easy: *castles, northern Germany.*

What about the names?

Lewis was Ludwig, and Jeffery was Gottfried. She didn't have to wait long. Both names came up. But Gottfried was important because a Count by that name owned property in Husum.

That was new information. But for now, she would focus on going to the bank with Thoren tomorrow.

CHAPTER NINETEEN

At the Bank

Amy was waiting at the entrance of the Kempinski Hotel when Thoren and his mother arrived. Julia's perfectly colored gray hair was wrapped around her head, without a strand out of place. Amy thought she looked as if she was going to meet the nation's president.

"We are heading north. The bank is in a tiny village north of Berlin. When Frederic left for South Africa, he put everything he valued in the safe-deposit box." She thought Thoren winked. "Do not worry; all of the papers should be there." He repeated *papier* in German for his mother, who nodded at the word.

As they got into the car, Amy asked how far they had to travel. Thoren replied, "Just up the road about forty miles, a little town—a village, really—called Wandlitz. It is a place no one would suspect Frederic would use."

He sighed. "Frederic wanted the box close to Berlin. Do not ask me why. His dead wife's home was in Sylt. When she was alive, they lived there most of the year. Happy times is what Frederic told me. He still owns the house. Said he kept it because of the good memories. He also liked to visit the islands."

The road was not an autobahn, but they still made good time. *Nobody driving in Germany pokes along*, thought Amy.

All the little villages were mirror images of what she thought Germany looked like a hundred years ago. Within an hour, they pulled into a village. No cobblestone streets, but everything else was old.

The bank was obvious: a small, neat, red-brick building sitting on the town square. Inside the bank were three teller stations and two desks in the center for bank officers. One of the officers stood up as Thoren handed him his identification. The officer typed up a paper. Thoren's mother signed, and the signature was verified. Everything was in order, and the officer took them to the locked vault with the safe-deposit boxes.

Opening the box was anticlimactic, but Thoren was right. The box was packed with papers. Fortunately, his mother had a large bag that held all the contents.

Thoren asked the officer a question, then spoke to Amy in English. "I told them that I wanted to close the box. But Frederic has paid in advance for ten more years."

"When did Frederic leave Germany?" asked Amy. It was a question she had wanted to ask for some time.

"Five years ago. He could be dead. My mother believes he is alive."

Amy found herself wondering what had really happened to Thoren's brother. Was Frederic in South Africa? If he was, then they should have been able to talk to him on the phone.

The drive back to Berlin was fast, and no one spoke. First, they dropped off his mother, who was still staying at her sister's, then they headed to Sonora's. The papers had to be reviewed and kept safe.

As they passed through the iron gate and drove up the graveled driveway to the front door, Thoren pointed to a monitor almost hidden in the trees on the side of the brown stucco mansion.

"Amy, that is the beauty of visual intelligence."

She looked at it and asked, "Thoren, when did you become an expert on this stuff?"

"It was a hobby, and my brother encouraged me."

"From South Africa?"

"No, when he lived here. We were always tinkering and kind of fell into it. At the time, it was unknown. Now, it has become something everyone knows about."

Amy knew that any high-tech gizmo would be right up Sonora's alley. Her aunt prided herself on having the latest security technology. It seemed to have failed with the bugging of her automobiles.

"How did you start working for my aunt?"

Thoren laughed, then explained. Again, it was his brother who knew some old Nazi general. The general had then introduced the two.

"I knew General Alfred von Hagen," said Amy as they pulled up to the door. "He knew my father and the Count."

Left unanswered was how Frederic knew the general.

CHAPTER TWENTY

Hunting for Gold in Zurich

The buffet was elegant, but Sonora was agitated. Amy could tell, as she kept rearranging the silk scarf around her neck.

"We need real information," Sonora said. "Thoren, you must finish translating Frederic's papers from the bank. Can you look them over tonight? Use my library. It's been cleared as safe, or declared 'clean'; that was the term the security team used."

Thoren took the papers and headed for the library. Ace started loading a plate from the buffet, and Amy followed. Sonora poured a scotch. She had more to say.

"Now for the gold. North of Berlin are dozens of places where the gold could have been stored. But before you head north, I have another search for you that might tie the north and the south together. My husband's private files are stored in our villa in Zurich. Amazingly, they've never been looked at. I just wasn't sure who to trust, so I ignored the files."

"They could hold the key," said Ace.

Sonora was always full of surprises, and tonight was no different. She told them her plane was ready to take them to Zurich in the morning. Amy and Ace looked at each other. Neither was surprised at their aunt's request to go to Zurich.

"No problem," said Ace, and Amy nodded.

"I'll keep an eye on what Thoren finds. Now, let's eat." Sonora picked up a plate and joined Ace at the buffet.

Amy ate a couple of pieces of beef and a salad, then was ready to return to the hotel. The Kempinski Hotel apartment seemed like an island in a city of questions whose answers went back before World War II.

• • •

The next morning, the fog was slowly lifting off the runway. Amy knew that small planes could take off in this weather, but she still worried. She heard a car engine and hoped it was Ace arriving. She had left early, and he followed in another taxi. Now, his taxi pulled up behind hers on the ramp to the airfield.

As Ace got out of the car, Amy laughed. Her cousin was wearing a brown monk's robe and sandals. "I'll explain on the plane to Zurich," said Ace as they boarded the plane.

They arrived in Zurich late morning and rented a car. Ace had the address and typed it into the navigation system. Within twenty minutes, despite the heavy traffic, they arrived at a tree-lined street with large stone mansions behind gated walls. Some might call them small palaces. The address was at the end of the street.

"Sonora told me," said Ace, "that there are two identical villas, with four apartments in each. One villa is for Lliessle Bank employees, the manager and his assistant. The other villa is a residence for the Lliessle family. They use two apartments for family and visitors, and the others are a records library and a general storage area."

"No computer?" asked Amy.

Ace laughed. "No, but they have internet, and I know in your luggage is a laptop. We should be comfortable staying in the villa for visitors. The staff at the other villa will bring in our meals. That will help us get through the records quickly. Luca, the Lliessle Bank manager, has made the arrangements—or so Sonora told me."

Ace pulled out a key. After opening the door, they entered a long hallway with walls filled with portraits of what she guessed were ancient Lliessle family members.

"The apartment is at the end of the hall." Ace had gotten the details from Sonora.

The keys worked easily, but everything worked in Switzerland. Inside Sonora's apartment were family pictures and some English antiques, with oriental carpets covering the hardwood floors. Amy looked at the pictures of her father and grandfather when they were young. And pictures of herself when she was a little girl. There were no pictures of her mother, which made sense since she had been a devoted Nazi. Nor were there pictures of either her grandmother or her grandfather's second wife, Sonora's mother, whom he had married late in life. Which was why Sonora was closer to her age and more like a sister than a step-aunt.

"Like a hotel, only more upscale. Let's check out the other apartment."

The second apartment looked like a very large library. The walls were filled with books and stacked boxes with dates on the front. In the middle of the main room was a couch and several desks with computers. Both Ace and Amy were wondering how in the world they would ever get through this information.

"I suggest," said Ace, "we start with the files for 1930 and work up to whatever year they stop."

Amy agreed. Ace seemed to know more about these papers than she did.

Two hours later, Amy and Ace had located the 1930s files and started to review the records year by year. They had gotten to 1932 with no mention of deposits or memos on gold. Then, they got lucky. They moved the boxes they had finished to one side and saw a piece of paper stuck to the bottom of a box.

Ace picked it up. "Bull's-eye. Call us lucky."

He handed Amy the invoice. Not only was it in English, but the invoice, stamped "508," also listed a number of bags of gold being transferred from a bank in Wurzburg, Germany, called the Bank of Business. He turned to the computer and clicked a few times.

"Wurzburg is a town in Bavaria, but the bank's home office is in Frankfurt. Branches of the Bank of Business are in every city across Germany, including Husum."

"So, they could send deposits anywhere," said Amy. Ace nodded.

After setting the invoice aside, they looked in the box. Several others in the box had the same code, 508, stamped at the top, but the banks and towns were different. The code saved them hours. Each took a box on either side of where they thought the paper had fallen out and found invoices in the boxes with the code 508 on every document. When they finished, they had a separate stack of boxes with the same code.

Ace picked up a box of 508s from 1941. It looked like all the invoices showed that gold had been deposited directly into the Lliessle Bank branch in Germany. For a moment, he was thankful that the boxes held only documents marked with the 508 code— real property deposits, or so the documents said at the top. What had happened to the other deposits? Someone had obviously re-viewed all the deposits and separated those with the code 508.

Thank God, he thought.

He started to pull the first invoice when Amy shouted, "I have a hit!" She showed Ace the 508 invoices. Printed on top were the words, in English, "bulk shipment," and in German, *"Der Hauptteil—Die Sendung."*

"These invoices, because they say 'bulk,' have to be the gold from the concentration camps that was melted into bars." He turned to an attached form in German. "This invoice says the gold bars were shipped to the Reich Norte Bank in Husum. I can read those words."

After flipping through other invoices, they could see that other bulk shipments were sent to German banks in Frankfurt and Berlin. Ace put his box on the floor and picked up a box labeled 1943. If the gold came from the concentration camps, then the box should be full of bulk shipments. It was. The first invoice and the remainder in the box labeled 1943 were shipped to Husum or Sylt Island. They both knew this was important.

"Amy, let's skim the boxes from 1941 to the end of the war—say 1945. We look for only bulk shipments to banks in Germany."

"I'm all in, Ace. Let's finish these files and fly back to Berlin. Looks like we'll be going to Husum tomorrow."

They started to review the documents in boxes with the code and noticed another similarity. Each document had a stamp. But what did the stamp mean?

"We'll ask Luca. He's been the Lliessle Bank manager for years. He may know what it means."

• • •

Over lunch and several bottles of wine and a bottle of scotch, the Lliessle Bank manager, Luca Favre, told them how the bank had been managed since the Count's death five years ago.

"Switzerland considered us a national bank with three branches. One here, of course, and one in Bern and one in Geneva." He paused, looking at the stamp Ace handed him. "The stamp is old and out-of-date. We do not use it today. It was used when the bank stamped new gold bars sent here from Germany."

He looked into his scotch glass. "Not a proud moment for those of us who are Swiss, but it is a fact. We took melted gold from jewelry and labeled the bars as if they had been in the Reichsbank in Berlin for years. The actual smelting of the gold was done in Poland."

"So, the Swiss shipped the bars," started Ace, "back to Berlin, the country of origin, after stamping them as 'Reichsbank'?"

"Yes."

"Any idea how much was shipped?"

"No one really knows," said Luca. "And the price of gold then isn't what it is today. Gold today is an immense fortune. What is important is most of it has yet to be found."

"They keep looking," said Amy.

Luca laughed. "In all the wrong places, searching lakes in Austria. I know the big find made in World War II was in the Merkers mine, but that was only about a billion, not including the artwork. My banking colleagues say that there is so much more. But where?"

He smiled at them. "Think about it. If you were a Nazi, would you leave it in Europe, or even in Switzerland? No. You would take it out. How? By submarine."

Ace was listening closely. "You're saying the gold would have been sent to places where subs could land."

"Right." Luca laughed. "More treasure hunters should have figured that out."

Amy and Ace looked at each other. Both knew it was time to return to Berlin. The next step was to go north.

"I wonder," said Amy, "what Thoren has found in Frederic's papers."

"Frederic?" said Luca. "The investment banker?"

Amy explained how Frederic's brother, Thoren, worked for Sonora and how, with his mother's help, they had opened Frederic's safe-deposit box. "Frederic has been in South Africa, but Thoren hasn't talked to him in some time."

Luca disagreed. He said Frederic had been seen in Zurich in the last month by several of the bank staff. "He is like a ghost. Was very close to the Count." He grinned. "I would guess that he is very close to the gold too. He was the one who sorted through the papers, who was working for the Lliessle Bank in Berlin before he disappeared. I never bought it that he went to South Africa. But then, what do I know?"

• • •

Bazyli Czartoryski never called without a reason. The Abbot picked up the phone, wondering what it could be.

"Abbot, Amy and Ace Prowers are in Zurich. Sonora opened the bank files. There is no telling what they might find."

The Abbot knew about the files that were archived in the Lliessle family home in Zurich. "Bazyli, you must know that Amy and Ace are looking for details on the stolen gold, on where it was hidden and who might have taken it out of Switzerland. Swiss bankers melted the gold from the concentration camps and numbered it as if it had come from the Reichsbank in Berlin. The Lliessle Bank did not keep it but sent the gold to Berlin, to the Reichsbank, and to German regional banks. Where the records are is a guess, if they exist at all."

Neither man said what he was thinking. The minute an outsider started looking at old bank records, the bankers would know that they were looking for the gold. So many groups in Germany and Austria had been doing that for years.

The Abbot went on to say that any records showing gold was transferred to a bank would be hard to find, even if they existed. "The records showing disbursements from the bank would be the ones to track. I bet those records could provide a starting point for where the gold had gone."

They both knew that the Reichsbank in Berlin shipped gold out of the city when the Allies begin to bomb it in late 1940. What couldn't be estimated was the amount of gold jewelry taken from concentration camps and later melted into gold bars. The bars were then stamped in Switzerland with the official seal from the Reichsbank.

"Bazyli, be assured, no one can prove whether a gold bar came from a bank transfer or from concentration camp victims."

"It is Frederic's fault," said Bazyli. "He took the gold and moved it out of our estate in Vilnius. But where to?"

The Abbot knew where—or could at least make a good guess. "To his wife's home in Husum, near Sylt Island. Today, a resort, yesterday, a secluded, out-of-the-way village."

"Abbot, if I hear the Prowers gang is heading to Husum, I am going after them."

Quietly, the Abbot said, "I understand."

Frederic had deceived him, misled him, lied. The Abbot had no loyalty to Frederic. And no reason to tell Bazyli that Frederic had moved the gold to Switzerland.

"Abbot, I need to know where they go to search for the gold. Frederic moved the gold from Vilnius, and then he disappeared. The gold had to go out by ship, or else it is hidden in northern Germany. If only we could find Frederic."

The Abbot agreed, then both fell silent. Neither knew where Frederic was, but both believed he was alive.

• • •

In Vienna, Bazyli was ready to move one of his teams north to Sylt Island. He needed the team to set up surveillance before the Prowers family arrived in Husum. It had to be Husum because that was the last town before the Danish border. He picked up the phone and called the training center.

"Sig, pick a team of four men. Get ready to send them to Sylt Island, and find a nice hotel or house for rent. Will sound like a holiday to them. They can mix with the tourists and await further instructions. I will get pictures of the Prowers family and Thoren for you. They will know who to follow. Wait for my call. It will be soon."

He thought for a moment. "And Sig, pick a man to follow Amy on her way to Husum. No telling what she might do along the way. Horst has been angling for a chance to use his skills. He might be the right one."

As he hung up, his mind went over what needed to be done. For now, there was nothing else.

CHAPTER TWENTY-ONE

In Zurich

Bob Morris looked up at the iron gate and back at the address Sonora had emailed to him. So, these were the Lliessle villas. To him, they were stone and cement palaces.

Typically Swiss, he thought. *Now, the search for the stolen gold begins.*

If retirement resulted in being fat, an excuse Ace always used, then Bob broke the mold. As tall as Ace, he looked the same as he had in Saudi Arabia: fit to take on the natives, as he used to say. Well, not quite. His hair had a lot of gray and sprinkles of white.

Simon Bell told him that the search would be complex. Bob knew Amy and Ace from their venture in Saudi Arabia.

After our time in Saudi, the three of us ought to be able to find the gold. Or am I just being naïve?

Sonora, the Abbot, and Simon Bell were contacts from his past. The Abbot had lived in East Berlin for decades and claimed his life in East Germany had not changed his political outlook, but Bob thought it had to have influenced him. One day, he was living in East Berlin, and the next day, he was in the West. Was he really a friend? Bob wasn't sure. He reached up and rang the bell on the iron gate.

Amy and Ace were delighted to see him. To Amy, Bob looked the same, with maybe a few more gray hairs.

"We were about to leave for Berlin and thought we'd see you there. What are you doing in Zurich?" Amy asked.

"Sonora wants me to look at the Count's personal bank files. No one has, and she thinks there might be some clues on the location of the gold." He went on to explain how, after he had retired from the CIA, a friend he had known since 1989 who worked in the German government asked him to help find the stolen Nazi gold.

"Once my friend Simon mentioned the stolen gold, *Raubgold*, I was hooked. I called Sonora, thinking she would have some contacts and information. What a surprise to find the two of you on this search. Simon is sure the gold is out there, somewhere in Europe. With all of us working on it, I know we'll find it. I need help with the background. Know a little, but tell me, what have you found in the Lliessle Bank records?"

Ace had to laugh. "Bob, your timing is perfect. We think we've figured out from bank records how gold transfers were made during the Third Reich. At least, we have some ideas.

Come with us to dinner. Luca, the Lliessle's bank manager, is an encyclopedia of information. We hope to learn more."

Luca was a Swiss from Italy and looked it. Short, with dark hair and dark eyes, and physically fit, his passion was hiking in the mountains. His knowledge about his country and the banking business did not disappoint them, nor did he question who Bob was. Working for the Count for years, he was used to foreigners arriving out of nowhere. As for the gold, he had lived with the gold stories all his life. Though Switzerland had made some reparations, he had always believed his government knew more about Nazi gold than the citizens had been told.

The meal was finished, and scotch was served, which Luca said was an old custom of the Count's. He took a sip and began his story.

"Switzerland maintained a policy of armed neutrality during both world wars, which was tricky business since the nations at war were on our border, and our populations spilled into these countries. I mean, we have Germans, French, Italians, and Austrians living here. The countries fighting each other found it convenient to use my country for diplomatic liaisons, for spying on each other, and, most importantly, for doing business. Business doesn't stop because of a war."

He continued on to say that because the country was centrally located and neutral, World War II built the Swiss banking industry. Equally important was that the country became a place where refugees and revolutionaries lived together.

"Few seem to remember," said Luca, "that Vladimir Lenin was shocked when socialist parties in Europe supported the First

World War. He moved to Switzerland in 1914 and stayed until 1917. After Tsar Nicholas II abdicated, he returned to Petrograd to lead the October Revolution in Russia."

He paused to sip his drink. "My country accepted over sixty-eight thousand wounded British, French, and German prisoners of war, who recovered from their injuries in mountain resorts. They were transferred from prisoner-of-war camps, which couldn't cope with the wounded. They spent the rest of the war in Switzerland. And that was the First World War. The Second World War is more complicated."

He looked around the room. "I hope there is enough scotch."

According to Luca, the history of secrecy in Swiss banking went back to the nineteenth century. In 1815, the Congress of Vienna formally approved Swiss neutrality. Originally, Switzerland was a place for wealthy European banks and aristocratic interests. Few knew that the Catholic French kings put their money in Swiss banks because they did not trust the Protestant banks.

During World War II, foreign accounts and the assets of countries were deposited in Swiss accounts. The Swiss saw secrecy as a way to build a banking empire. After the war, the international community tried to open these accounts. But to the Swiss, secrecy was an unwritten code like that of doctors or priests. The Swiss saw a need for offshore financial accounts, tax havens, in places like the Cayman Islands and the Bahamas, and they took advantage of it.

As Luca took a sip of his drink, Bob interrupted. "I read somewhere that a few years ago, maybe in 2018, it was estimated that Swiss banks held a quarter of all the assets that crossed borders. The Caribbean and Dubai are tax havens, but Switzerland is the number one choice of the wealthy citizens of the world."

"*Ja*," said Luca, "we are a nation of mountains. Underground vaults, old military bunkers, are used to store gold, silver, diamonds, and anything else they want. The Swiss government has never required the vaults to have the same standards as the banks."

Luca paused, then continued, "A selling point for the vaults is they are as secure as a bank, without the regulations. In the last twenty years, storage areas have been sold to Swiss banks, to private citizens, and to corporations. Sales started during World War II, when wealthy citizens set up accounts in the banks and bought storage areas."

He smiled and sipped his drink. "It is ironic. The Swiss banking laws of 1934 protected Jewish assets and also protected the assets of the Nazis who stored their gold and cash. Hitler is said to have had an account of over a million reichsmarks."

Ace walked around the room with a bottle, keeping everyone's glasses of scotch full.

Bob seemed to know a lot about Swiss banking laws. "All I know is that after the war, some progress was made to break the secrecy of banks."

"*Ja*," said Luca. "We see that as an attack on our culture. I don't personally feel that way, but my countrymen do. Since 1990, we have been one of the world's top tax havens."

"I read somewhere," said Amy, "that the Swiss are serious about the quality of their chocolate, the accuracy of their watches, and the secrecy of their banks."

"Quite right," said Luca. "You see, my country was no match for Germany's military. But Germany needed a way to pay neutral countries for war materials. Payments in Swiss francs were made to Sweden for iron ore, to Portugal for manganese used in gun barrels, to Turkey for chromium for ball bearings. Swiss banks never asked where the Reich got the gold. None of the other countries ever touched any gold. The raw materials were paid for in Swiss francs. Over the years, the Swiss have invested in real estate, in insurance, and in stocks."

Luca went on, "A little-known fact is that even before the war began, Sweden provided over forty percent of the iron ore for Germany's war machine. We Swiss also supplied guns to the Reich, with the last order delivered in April 1945."

Luca stopped to take a sip of scotch. "As a Swiss citizen, I am not proud of what happened in World War II, but today, our economy is strong because of what happened. We have no raw materials yet today are rated second only to Dubai in per capita income."

"Didn't the Swiss prolong the war by paying other countries in Swiss francs for their raw materials?" asked Amy. But she was really thinking about the estimates she had read that seventy to eighty-five million people on both sides died during the war.

How many lives, she wondered, *could have been saved if raw materials had not been sold to the Reich?*

Luca nodded. "You make a good point, though most of the gold transfers were done in 1943, which was the year when the Nazis lost the war. When Hitler invaded Russia and was defeated at the battle of Stalingrad in 1943, high-ranking Nazis and others in the know, usually SS men, realized Germany could not win. They took advantage of their country's arrangements with my country. Nazis, and especially the SS, set up personal accounts. I do not like to say this, but it is true. Many, if not most, of those accounts have never been used since the war and are still open."

Bob spoke again, showing more knowledge of the countries involved. "In 1939, Germany was busted. The Reichsbank had nothing in its coffers. In each country the Nazis conquered, the first thing they did was to raid the national bank of that country and transfer the gold to the Reichsbank in Berlin. If I remember correctly, the raided banks were in Albania, Austria, Belgium, Czechoslovakia, Greece, Luxembourg, the Netherlands, Poland, and Yugoslavia.

"A director at the Reichsbank came up with the ingenious idea of dead man's gold. These were accounts opened at the Reichsbank for concentration camp prisoners, primarily those in Auschwitz, where over a million died. The money was then transferred to the private accounts of high-ranking members of the Nazi Party."

Amy, who had been listening to the discussion, said, "Bob, a lot of that gold would have gone north. All history seems to talk about is the gold going south to Merkers mine or to Bavaria."

Amy looked at Ace. "This is making the case for going north. Bob, we're on our way back to Berlin and intend to head north. Come with us?"

Bob shook his head. "Too many skeletons in my closet, but if I'm persuaded, what can I say? Now, Ace, your monk's outfit inspires me. You should go to Austria and meet Bazyli Czartoryski. Bazyli will be looking for the gold too. If you can become part of his team, we could learn what he is doing to find it. Simon has a contact that knows you. Marton is his name. I think he did translations for Vince and your father. You can't just come off the street and tell a guy like Bazyli, 'Yeah, I want to lie, kill, spy for you.'"

"No problem," said Ace, to which they all laughed.

"Marton can be a big help in getting you in Bazyli's group. Translated, that means Bazyli will kill Marton if you screw up. Just kidding, but you get the idea."

Amy listened to Bob and thought about the elderly monk killed in Vilnius. She knew Ace. Her cousin was a magnet for anything involving danger.

Bob spoke like the expert he was. "Bazyli's group is the next generation of Nazis, and they have to be looking for the gold. And they have to be watching what Amy is going to do."

"He makes sense, Amy," said Ace. "I should go to Vienna, and you should go to Husum. Sonora can send Thoren with you. Frederic had to be involved. Thoren would know better than anyone what his brother might have done. We—and that means you too, Bob—should fly back to Berlin tomorrow and bring Sonora up to speed."

"I give up," said Bob. "But I will not talk in her house. I know it was swept by her security staff, but there still could be a bug."

"So, how do we get it clean?" asked Amy.

Bob had the answer. He'd ask Simon Bell, his German friend in the security service, to have his people double-check the house and cars. "It's the best we can do. Until then, keep important chats outside."

"Will you stay in Berlin at Sonora's home?"

"No, I'll stay at the Adlon-Kempinski because the location is central. Maybe just a day, and then I'll fly back to Switzerland. Sonora has to have more information about the gold—and certainly about gold storage facilities here in Switzerland. Her knowledge can save me a lot of time."

Amy and Ace looked at each other. "Gold storage facilities?" asked Amy.

"Something new all the time," said Ace.

"I know where some of them are," said Luca. "But the problem is getting into the storage facilities. They are . . . how you say . . . impregnable."

"That's what I've been told," said Bob. "But didn't Count Lliessle often go to visit the storage facilities?"

Luca grimaced. "Marton's father usually accompanied him. They took nothing with them and returned with nothing. Seemed odd at the time, but I was busy with the bank."

For a moment, there was silence, all of them thinking the same thing. Where were the Count's storage facilities? Did Sonora know how to get into the storage facilities? Did Lliessle Bank have a storage vault? The answer to that had to be yes.

Bob broke the silence. "Whatever's in the storage facilities, I'll find out after I visit Sonora. No bullion vaults are impregnable, even in Switzerland."

He spoke confidently, but everyone listening wondered if it really could be that easy.

Plotting in Berlin

Sonora was impressed with what Amy and Ace had found in Zurich with the bank transfers, but to her, the map was more important. She came back from the sitting room in the front of the house, carrying the old map. Only a few knew that innocuous room had a safe embedded in the wall, as secure as in any bank.

"Ace, all we could recognize was Berlin. I hope you can enlighten Amy and myself on what else might be on the map. Bob would have been here, but he's meeting his German friend Simon Bell. Tomorrow, he flies back to Zurich, and before he leaves, I'm meeting him for lunch at the Kempinski. He has his work cut out for him to find the storage facility, if there is one. I don't really know how I can help."

Out of his knapsack, Ace pulled a colored map of northern Germany. "Got this at a shop at the airport. It'll show us where roads are today. We compare the old map Vince found to this current map." To Sonora and Amy, it seemed like it would work.

The dining room was laid out buffet style with platters of ham, beef, smoked salmon, and salads. A side table had a selection of fine red and white wines, all German, and another smaller one held desserts. They moved some of the food aside and opened up the two maps side by side on the buffet.

Looking at the colored map, Amy saw castles, rivers, lakes, and canals north of Berlin. To her, these were places where the gold could be stored, waiting for a ship or a plane to take it out of the country.

Ace took the lead. "Because gold is heavy, it had to be taken out by ship. Or it could have been taken out bit by bit to Norway on planes, and from there, on a ship. It had to be stored somewhere."

Ace sounded confident.

Why does gold always get men focused? Amy wondered.

Then, Sonora reinforced his confidence. "The Third Reich collapsed much sooner than the leaders thought. In fact, it ended abruptly, considering the war had gone on for five years. Once the Allies crossed the Rhine River, resistance disappeared. The top leaders on all sides were surprised.

"The Russian guns pounded Berlin from the east. The Germans headed west, preferring to surrender to the Americans than to the Russians. General George Patton was sweeping across the center of Germany. His army cut off the retreat by the

Nazi leaders to the south. Anyone who left before the Americans arrived got out. Where would the rest go?"

"North," said Ace.

Sonora nodded. "Right, and there was no resistance north. The air war was nonexistent. After five years of fighting, the Russians were tired. What no one remembers is that everyone was tired, including the Allies, the German military, and the German civilian populations. People forget that a war doesn't stop at five o'clock. It's twenty-four seven.

"The top Nazi leadership thought they had more time. The idea that the gold was sent north makes sense. It could have been stored between Berlin and Rjukan, the German airbase in Norway. Believe it or not, the Nazis were still active in Norway."

She paused before making her point. "Why travel across Europe when you can leave by going north? The Nazis had seaplanes based in Rjukan, Norway. Those planes could be refueled at sea by submarines, or else the gold could be loaded on the submarines in northern Germany." She adjusted her necklace and sipped her scotch. "Someone has to know where it is."

Amy wasn't sure. "It has been over seventy years. Who could still be alive?"

"No one," said Sonora. "I hate to bring this up, but I, for one, have always believed that Hitler and a number of high-ranking Nazis made it out of Berlin to South America. To form the Fourth Reich, they needed financing to support not only their lifestyles but also their dreams.

"The Count always thought that many senior Nazis escaped, not just on the well-traveled ratline through Italy and Spain run by the Vatican but also by going north. In Argentina, the dictator Juan Perón provided support for them, as he had during the war. But to start new, they needed money." She paused again. "Gold was funneled through Swiss banks during the war. The Count told me that he handled some of those transfers."

"Right," said Ace, not sounding surprised at all. Amy could see that Ace was on board with what Sonora said. And she agreed Sonora made sense. But Ace wasn't finished.

"Gold is heavy, and we're talking about tons. The seaplanes could have flown the eight thousand miles to South America, using submarines for refueling. Or, if the gold went by ship, again, submarines could refuel them."

Ace told a story about one seaplane that arrived in Uruguay and crashed in the bay outside Luna de Roche. About forty senior Nazis with bodyguards were seen on the beach, waiting for the engine to be repaired. When it was, the plane was on its way to Argentina.

Ace, between chewing bits of beef and ham, pointed out that Frederic's papers might hold a clue. "Why was Frederic so protective of his papers? Thoren said that he was obsessed with the stolen Nazi gold. He only took the South Africa assignment because his company gave him an important promotion. I hope Thoren finds something we can use in his brother's papers."

Amy was looking at the map when she noticed Ace had moved over to the computer. He said, "Give me a place, any place. I'll pull it up and see what the computer says about its history. Maybe it will help us decide where to go."

"Sounds good," said Amy. "Going north on the map, the first town is Schwerin. It's by a lake and has a canal that empties into the Baltic Sea. No airfield is shown on either map." She spelled *Schwerin* for him.

"Here's what the computer says about the area. It's about two hours driving time north of Berlin." He read quickly.

Schwerin was considered one of the old Romantic Road cities. There was a castle on an island in the lake, a museum with a Rubens, and a Gothic church, and it had a festive, old-world atmosphere that tourists loved.

"Too much visibility," said Amy, and she looked back at the map.

Farther north, she saw the town of Keil, which had a canal and an airfield. The gold could be flown north to Norway. Surely, someone on the Allied side was watching these areas, and she said so.

"You're right to think that, Amy," said Sonora, "but at the time, the Allies were focused on Berlin and on central Germany. Little attention was paid to Hamburg or any of the areas in northern Germany. The province, called Mecklenburg, ended up in the Russian zone, but the Russians were exhausted from fighting and ignored entire towns in this northern area. It would have been easy to get gold out by ship or by airplane."

Ace agreed. "Amazingly, there was no air cover by the Allies. They didn't have the resources and counted on the navy to blockade any ships." He seemed to know what he was talking about.

"I, for one," said Sonora, "am frustrated because there has to be someone living in Berlin who knows what happened to the gold. The Reichsbank gold was found in the Merkers mine, or so the experts say. I don't believe it was all there. The Nazis had gold from other countries, from national banks, and from melting down gold from teeth and jewelry from the prisoners in the death camps. The Russians were coming, but they were on the main roads, so the gold had to go north, or even east."

Amy asked what she thought they should do. Sonora knew that checking out the deposits in the Husum bank was important. But Amy knew that her aunt wanted to get all the information possible before exploring the towns.

"The Abbot has to know more than he's let on," said Sonora. "He was in the monastery the entire war, and then in the years when the Russians controlled East Germany. I guess as a praying monk. His prayers seem to have been in vain, but what else was he into? He was ducking bombs throughout the war. Wonder whose side he was praying would win and whose side he's on today?" Then, she stopped. "I worry that if we meet the Abbot, we may give him more information than we get. I don't trust him. But I know we must see him."

Ace asked, "Do you trust Marton?"

Her reply startled them. "Maybe."

Amy was looking at the journal where she had seen the two names written in the margin: Gottfried and Ludwig. Almost to herself, she said the names aloud. Ace at the computer heard her and typed *Gottfried* in.

"Hey, got a hit on Gottfried. Someone with that name had a castle and an estate outside Husum. A Count Gottfried owned a lot of land and was the last of his line of German nobility. His land would be a place to store gold, with no one really watching."

Amy thought they might be making a mistake. "From what I read, today, it's a tourist spot. Though, it seems there are miles of mudflats along the beach."

They heard a car pull up. Amy was sure it was Thoren. "Let's see if he found anything from going through Frederic's papers from the safe-deposit box."

Moments later, Thoren joined them. Sonora told him to take a plate from the buffet and eat something.

"Thoren, in the car, with her limited English, your mother mentioned a house that Frederic owned outside of Husum that's on the water," said Amy.

"Yes, the house belonged to his dead wife. Her family was part of the estate of Count Gottfried, and they got the house. All the years since her death, Frederic paid taxes on the property. He also had a bank account in Husum. The water up there is really just mudflats. Before her father died, his wife's family had a dredging service. I mean, the bay is mudded all year round up there. After her death, the boat, the platform, and the dredge were in a boat shed behind the house. The papers from his box in the bank included account numbers for the bank in Husum and a key to the safe-deposit box in the Husum bank."

To make his point, Thoren pulled an envelope containing keys out of his pocket. "The keys to the box at the bank in Husum. Who knows what it holds?"

Ace asked, "What are you all thinking?"

"A dredge could carve a channel through the mudflats, deep enough for a submarine or a fishing trawler to get close to shore and to load the gold," said Thoren.

Thoren looked at the map on Sonora's table. "I can make this simple," he said. "Frederic did not try to hide anything. He tied all the deposit slips to the Husum property or to a bank in Husum. Look at the slips, and you will see that gold labeled 'bulk shipments' went to the house and the rest went to the bank. The bank sent him monthly statements until he left for South Africa. Then, they stopped. He may have told the bank to hold them. That was five years ago—when he left. The statements showed his account then was over a million euros."

Before anyone could comment, Thoren said, "The house is on a large tract of land. The dredge is still on their land. Frederic's notes indicate that his wife's family had a visit from the Nazis during World War II. His wife's father was the son of Count Gottfried. He was a right-winger and an early Nazi supporter."

Ace and Amy looked at each other.

"Could Gottfried, the name Vince wrote in the margins of the journal, have been a director at the London Bank?" asked Amy.

Thoren shrugged. "Do not know, but it could be true."

Sonora interjected that it was starting to make sense.

Thoren continued. "No one is too sure if, or wants to admit, her family was pro-Nazi. It is very likely that her father was a Nazi and could have had a prominent position in administration in northern Germany, like in Husum. Today, no one wants to talk about what happened during the war, and few who knew the truth are alive. They cannot really take gold out of the small airport in Husum; the sea has to be the route, using the dredge to open a channel through the mudflats."

He went on to say that in the safe-deposit box were bank statements from a second bank in Husum, showing two more accounts with balances of over fifty million euros. While Frederic was the primary account holder, all the accounts had multiple names, including Thoren, their mother, and Fredric's long-dead wife. Access wasn't easy. It took a key and a password.

Thoren held up a pouch with the items in it. "Right in here. They were in his safe-deposit box. How Frederic got our signatures on all of the accounts, my mother's and mine, I have no idea. Maybe he faked them. But what he did allows me to get into all the safe-deposit boxes in Husum."

Sonora and Amy looked at each other.

"Amy, I think you and Thoren need to get to Husum. Ace, I think Vienna is in your future," said Sonora.

She got up and walked to a closed wooden cabinet and pressed the wall next to it. As the wall swung inward, the other side slid out. It held a rack of weapons. Taking out four handguns, she turned to Amy and Thoren.

"Just in case. Take the ammo too; you never know what you might need. I hope you don't have to use them, but it pays to be prepared."

"Sonora, I am impressed," said Ace. "But if I should go to Bazyli's, better if he gives me a gun."

Amy was looking at the guns. "Thoren, how about a shotgun or one of the military-style rifles?"

"An AK-47 is all we need, since they are easy to use," said Thoren.

Amy said she needed to pack; Thoren always had a bag ready to go. He learned to keep a bag ready, working for Sonora.

Amy was thinking about Count Gottfried. That was one of the names Vince had written in the margins of the journal. Was there a tie between Frederic's wife and where the gold was? To her, that was possible, but today, with everyone dead, did it matter? Maybe it mattered only if Frederic was alive.

• • •

Bob Morris had delayed his flight to Zurich to meet with Simon Bell. Fortunately, the airlines flew from Berlin several times a day. When he entered the airline's first-class lounge, he saw Simon dressed in a suit, with his gray hair slicked back. Bob ordered a single malt scotch and another for Simon.

He quickly came to the point of the meeting. "Simon, I need your help in getting Marton to introduce Ace to Bazyli Czartoryski. We need to find out what he knows about the gold. I think Ace can find that out if he's part of Bazyli's group in Austria."

Simon agreed. "Marton can get him in. He has good credentials for joining Bazyli's group. He might even improve the men's military skills. Many of those guys need a lot of training. Not in how to kill but in how to get information without killing."

With that comment, Bob knew that Simon's organization was keeping an eye on the Czartoryski family. Bob said he thought Bazyli had spent a fortune getting his covert operations team together.

Simon laughed. "He did, but Bob, you have to recruit the right type of guys. Bazyli can make money in his businesses, but that does not mean he knows how to run teams. Teams that are in training for God knows what."

Bob said, "Simon, what is a quandary is no one seems to know where the gold is."

Simon's response surprised him, though he knew it could be true. "Suppose, Bob, it is all gone." He paused. "But the amount that has been found and the amount that may be out there make it worth the time of gold hunters. My country and other countries here in Europe certainly have enough of those hunters." He pulled out a card and handed it to Bob. "Marton will be expecting Ace to call."

Watching Bob leave, Simon wondered if the American knew that Marton was a *blénder*. But did it really matter? Marton was being used by all sides. He hoped the young man knew what he was doing.

CHAPTER TWENTY-THREE

Czartoryski Home Outside Vienna

Bazyli Czartoryski looked at Marton. "I feel like I am cursed. My son died in Nuremberg, which was enough of a sacrifice for our movement. Now, tell me what the Prowers are up to and what you can do about them."

Marton understood Bazyli's frustration but seemed to miss the point. "We have to wait. I believe the search for the gold is about to intensify."

"Wait!" shouted the Russian millionaire. "You were part of the old Stasi. The East Germans knew how to handle situations like this. You should too."

"We will get the gold. I promise," said Marton. He knew that the old man was volatile—even more so with his son dead. Uwe had been his favorite, though Marton never could understand why.

They looked at each other, and Bazyli put his head in his hands. "*Ja, ja.* Call me when you have their plans."

"I will," replied Marton.

Bazyli watched the German walk down the steps of his villa and into the waiting car. His private jet would take Marton back to Berlin. He knew he had to avenge his son. That was what his family had always done. It was an eye for an eye.

Now, thought Bazyli, *it is my time to strike.*

He opened a drawer in his desk and pulled out a box of Cuban cigars. As he smoked, he looked out the window at the extensive grounds of his villa. He enjoyed this residence more than the one in Vilnius that his family had fled during World War II. Being on the outskirts of Vienna had its appeal. For one thing, the sun shone in Austria more than farther north.

North, he puffed on his cigar, *is where I want to be with my team.*

He wouldn't leave Austria but would send a team north to follow the Prowers family. His gut told him the gold had gone north.

Now is the time for the Grey Eagles to show their worth.

He pulled out his pocket watch. It was noon. The Grey Eagles should be training on the east side of the villa grounds. The walk would do him good.

As he walked, he remembered how Vilnius looked toward the end of the war. He was just a small boy when his father told him that the family was leaving for Austria. Everyone—the military, the civilians—was tired from the bombing and the raids from the Russians on the east and the Germans on the west.

A cavern ran beside the Vilnius home, and it had been reinforced with concrete. His father made it clear that it was off-limits, which, to him, made it all the more interesting. One day, he cut between the hedges and crawled down under the trees to an air outlet. It was just big enough for him to climb into.

With his pocket light, he saw that the cavern was full of rows of what looked like bricks, stacked as tall as he was. He picked one up, dusted it off, and peered at the inscription: "Reichsbank," followed by a number. He knew that the stack was gold bullion because the color shone through the dust covering it.

A month or so later, if his memory served him—and his always did—a troop of SS arrived with a couple of trucks. They talked to his father and took the gold away. Since he wasn't supposed to go into the cavern, he couldn't ask his father where they were taking the bars.

He realized that there was only one goal; the Grey Eagles needed to find out where the trucks had taken the gold so many years ago. Was it even possible? Their mission was clear: following the Prowers clan, or whoever else Sonora had lined up, made sense. One team, four men, was all that was needed.

He stopped walking to relight his cigar. His role was critical. Once they found the gold, it would have to be guarded and moved to a safe location. The problem was that they didn't know the location of the gold, and until they did, he couldn't make any plans.

Taking it to Switzerland was a neon light to the German government. They were watching him, even though he lived in Austria. He couldn't see hauling gold across Germany or across any of the European Countries.

The gold must be in northern Germany, where it could be moved on ships or on submarines to South America, he thought.

Up ahead, he saw the Grey Eagles running on the track. Not a good time to visit. The last thing he wanted to do was to disrupt training.

Siegfried—or Sig, as he was called—motioned him over to a shaded table. He was the leader as well as the trainer. Bazyli would have preferred something alcoholic but took the fruit juice cocktail, smiling.

"Sorry, sir," said Sig. "It is all we have."

"I know, no problem. Sig, I think it is time to send the team north. Only you will know the real purpose. Like we talked before, they should think of it as a paid vacation."

Sig understood the history and the talents needed on the team. "The men I have picked have overlapping skills and can swim and scuba dive. I think we need four men. That way, we will have some backup. Have found a nice beach house on Sylt Island."

Bazyli was pleased. Sig was one employee on his payroll who had his total confidence.

Catching a ride back to the house, Bazyli realized he needed to touch base with the Abbot. Working with the Stasi could corrupt anyone. The Abbot had spent too many years with the East German leadership. Like Marton, the Abbot didn't inspire confidence. He hoped the Abbot wasn't at some retreat.

When Bazyli arrived home, he went to a locked bookcase in his study and took out a burner phone. He didn't know if the German secret service was tapping the monastery's phone, but likely, the phones at his villa were tapped by the Austrians. No guess what else might be. Sweeps were done weekly. Every so often, bugs were caught, usually after a visit from an electrician or a plumber.

The Abbot answered on the first ring. "I know it is you, my friend. We have had a lot of calls lately." Bazyli was pleased he didn't use his name. "Pretty sure we are in the clear," said the Abbot.

Now, Bazyli went into the type of nontalking they did when something was important. He asked about the Prowers family and whether they were going on vacation. Translated, that meant that the family was looking for the gold.

"They are still plotting where to go."

To Bazyli, that was good news. It meant that the Prowers did not have a destination.

Then, the Abbot said north, but he wasn't sure where. "I wish I could be more specific."

"No problem," said Bazyli. "Be in touch if something comes up."

He hung up and called Sig. They needed one of the men who could work on his own to follow the Prowers group north. He needed to keep track of what Amy was doing and where she was going.

• • •

The Abbot hung up and thought for a moment. He opened his desk drawer and pulled out a map of northern Germany. His mind went back to the days after World War II, when he was a young monk.

The Allies had no air power to cover northern Germany. They were focused on the center of the country, where the German army was located. Today, everyone seemed to forget that radar coverage was nonexistent. That fact was why he thought Hitler had escaped from the bunker by plane.

When he was a young monk in the monastery, strangers would come to visit the old Abbot. He was the one to usher them into the meeting. One day after their visit, the old Abbot told him that the war had not ended.

"The Reich lives on."

As a young monk, he couldn't ask what the old Abbot meant. Today, Czartoryski was saying the same things. The term "neo-Nazi" could not be used in Germany, but it was used in America. Bazyli called the right-wing group the Grey Eagles, but the Abbot knew they were Nazis. He also knew that none of them would give up until they found the rest of the gold.

He thought about the amount of gold. Twenty billion taken from twelve countries' state banks and stored in the Reichsbank in Berlin. About nine billion was found by the Americans in the Merkers mine in southern Germany. Three hundred million was siphoned off for operations in Argentina before the war. So, that left half, almost ten billion. Some had to go to Switzerland to pay neutral countries like Sweden and Portugal that had supported the Nazi war effort.

Finally, there was the gold jewelry taken from the camps, from the Holocaust victims. This was melted down and re-branded by the Swiss to look as if the bars came from the Reichsbank. He remembered that Bazyli used to say, "Look at three million married couples and their wedding rings. How much is that gold?" No one knew or could seem to calculate the worth.

Looking down at the map, the Abbot recalled his last conversation with Frederic before he left for South Africa. The young man worked for a brokerage house in Berlin and had assisted with monastery finances. He came to the monastery because he wanted the Abbot's opinion of Goering's and Himmler's estates north of Berlin. Frederic wanted to know if the gold could have been stored at these locations.

Frederic told him that he had asked Bazyli if he could be a Grey Eagle. Bazyli told him not now, but maybe later when he was back from South Africa. The Abbot thought it was something more. The request to join the group was a diversion to make Bazyli wonder about his true affiliation. The Abbot was sure of that.

The problem was that if Frederic had the gold, where did he hide it? Neither he nor Bazyli knew the answer.

CHAPTER TWENTY-FOUR

Translating the Papers

The hotel phone rang at six in the morning. Amy picked it up and heard Ace's voice. "Hope you're packed. Sonora has a private jet ready to take you north. I'll ride with you to the airport. You'll never guess what she wants me to do."

Amy was glad she had packed a small bag the night before, and she arrived at the lobby just behind Ace.

"What's happening?" she asked as they got into a cab.

"Change in plans. Sonora called me a few minutes to six. Bob convinced her that I should make contact with the neo-Nazi groups. Says I make the perfect candidate for membership. And he's arranged for Marton to make the introduction.

We'll be bonding with the neo-Nazis—oh, I mean the German right-wingers," said Ace.

Thoren met them at the private airfield north of Berlin. As they waited to board the small plane and for the pilots to arrive, he told Amy and Ace more of what he learned in his brother's files.

"I had information I did not know I had. Beside Frederic's wife's land and the house, there is a graveyard, including a crypt. Seems that during the war, the crypt was enlarged. Since it is on the edge of the graves, a truck can pull right up to the crypt."

He continued with a story that defied belief. Frederic's notes included a dinner that he and his wife had with a local mortician who dug graves and provided gravestones. The man was a good friend of his father-in-law, Count Gottfried.

The mortician told the couple that near the end of the war, on two occasions, trucks came up and off-loaded coffins into the enlarged crypt. He was asked to put up new headstones, never sure whether there were any bodies in the coffins. Over the years, he had been curious, but he was an old man. It was best to leave what was in the graves at rest.

"When the mortician died," said Thoren, "he was buried next to those graves."

"Everyone is dead today, right?" asked Amy.

"Yes, but Frederic's notes tell us where to look."

"Now," said Amy, "we know why Frederic kept the property and paid the taxes. Wonder what we'll find."

She looked at Ace, who said, "I wish I was coming with you."

"Ace, you know I'm fine on my own, and Thoren is both a bodyguard and tour guide. Right?"

"I am," said Thoren.

"We'll stay in touch, Ace. And I want to hear from you too." Amy waved goodbye as they walked to the plane.

Just under three hundred miles to Husum. In the jet, they would be there in time for dinner. She couldn't allow herself to think beyond that.

CHAPTER TWENTY-FIVE

Still in Berlin

Marton looked at the people walking down the Kurfürstendamm, the main shopping street in Berlin. Simon had picked a place where, in Marton's eyes, half of Berlin was shopping and eating. He saw Simon sitting at the back of an outdoor coffeehouse.

They exchanged greetings, and Marton ordered a coffee. Simon got to the point at once. "I take it the documents center in Nuremberg was a bust?"

"Simon, you know how much information is there. I would need a month to go through it all. And Bazyli wanted to see me in Vienna."

"Can you get back into Sonora Lliessle's house?" asked Simon.

Marton thought for a moment and then said doing research for her was his connection, so the answer was yes. "All I have to say is that I found a connection to the Nazi gold. That should work."

Then, Simon told Marton that he needed to introduce Sonora's nephew Ace to Bazyli.

"I know Ace. Have seen him over the years when he visited Sonora and the Count in Berlin. Should not be a problem. He is a straight shooter and has a background in the military. To be honest, Bazyli can use him," said Marton.

Marton left Simon sipping his coffee. Simon remembered a classmate, a good friend from his university days, who had worked for the German version of the FBI. When he retired, he went to Husum, where his family had a hotel. Klaus Meyer was a good agent. He would give him a call.

CHAPTER TWENTY-SIX

In Vienna

Sig looked puzzled. "Boss, what are we supposed to find at Husum?"

Bazyli smiled. "Maybe nothing. Just keep Amy in your sight in case she finds something. Frederic could have hidden the gold anywhere."

Sig thought for a moment. "Is the gold really up there? I mean, everyone is looking in the lakes and mountains that border Austria."

Bazyli laughed. "The truth is that no one knows where it is. But what is certain is that the Nazi gold is still in Germany. Some of the gold made it to Argentina during the war, but by now, it has been spent. Sig, they have to be desperate. My family had a large inheritance, but most of the families that supported the Third Reich did not have money or property. Part of our fortune was the family gold stored on our family estate outside Vilnius. Fortunately, my father got the gold out of Vilnius before the Russians arrived. That is what is stored in the cave."

Sig had seen the stack of bars in the cave. Now, he knew the family had brought their gold with them when they moved during the war. He knew that was the Czartoryski personal fortune, not the Nazi gold.

"Do not tell the team. Gold changes men, makes them greedy. We will say that Frederic had a few gold bars that belonged to my father before the war. That is only a very small part of what Amy Prowers and Thoren are trying to find."

For a moment, Bazyli allowed himself to look worried. Then, the look was gone. "Those two are not your biggest problem. Right-wing radicals, the Alternative for Germany, AfD, are looking for the gold, and they are the problem."

He paused. They both knew that they could not control German politics.

"Back to Husum. Fishing . . . have the team be on a fishing trip. Buy the rods and reels here. Arriving at Husum, they will look like zealots. If anyone asks why they came up, say for the saltwater fishing, a change from the deep-water lakes in Austria. The local folks will recognize their accents as Austrian. In fact, the more I think about it, hire a boat, one with a big engine. We want to be prepared for whatever the Prowers group does."

Sig agreed. "What about this Prowers guy that Marton is bringing today as a potential recruit?"

Bazyli laughed. "Go slowly. We have to evaluate him as a person—and the skill set he has. I mean, he is Sonora's nephew, and I do not want her pissed at me. His background is impressive, spending years with a secret US Special Forces unit. Seems like he would fit right in."

"We can use more men who have had specialized training," said Sig. "Some of the military men we have recruited are poorly trained."

"You are right, Sig. The new guy could get them up to speed."

• • •

Ace wanted to spend a day in Vienna, seeing the sights, but Marton said they were expected at Bazyli's estate.

"We can visit it later. You could be here for months. The city is not going anywhere," said Marton.

"I know concentrating on the training will come first. That is, after I convince Bazyli that I'm committed to his cause." Ace sounded resigned to his role.

Marton said that Ace's background in Special Forces groups would help integrate him into the group and added, "You are right. You must show the level of political intensity that all these right-wingers have. Show them that your politics are their politics. Sonora has a reputation for being more of a right-winger than most know. You are her nephew. Show them that you share her political beliefs."

Ace said nothing, since he wasn't sure what his aunt's politics were.

"We are almost there," said Marton. "This is the main gate."

A large country home, or what some would call a modest castle, waited for them at the end of the driveway. Trees surrounded the mansion, with small gravel roads running down both sides of the main road into the forest.

"Bazyli has a huge training facility in the woods. It includes a running track and a shooting range."

"Do we live in barracks?" asked Ace. Though, as he spoke, he realized it didn't matter. When training was over, they would be out in the countryside, very likely staying at safe houses or at hotels.

All Marton knew was that wherever they stayed would be comfortable. Bazyli spared no expense on his men. He pulled up in front of the house.

"The real issue is for you to convince these right-wingers that you are one of them. I do not think they will give you a test, but you have to show hatred of immigrants. And most important, you have to convince them you believe in white supremacy. That you are an Aryan. Should not be too hard, as you have the height and head structure."

"My weight is the problem. I've never been thin, but I didn't used to be so heavy," said Ace.

"You should be okay. A lot of Germans are overweight. All that beer, you know."

Ace didn't add that he wasn't looking forward to some work regime to lose weight but rationalized that if he needed to, he would.

As they got out of the car, the fourteen-foot wooden door opened, and a tall, bald man motioned them in. He was the house manager. Bazyli was running late but said for them to wait. The red wine the manager served made the wait worthwhile.

"Austrian wine?" asked Ace.

Both Marton and the manager laughed.

"Austria does have vineyards, but Bazyli prefers French wine," said the manager.

He was pouring another glass for them when Bazyli arrived, apologizing for his late arrival. "I decided to fly in from Budapest. Fog delayed flights, and it would have been faster to drive."

After a couple of sips of wine, Ace could see that he was all business.

"Mr. Prowers, you come highly recommended, but I am concerned about your aunt's politics. Sometimes, she supports the AfD Party in Germany, other times not. Austria has its own parties, but the AfD in Germany is the dominant player in all right-wing policies. Some are confused by the AfD—Alternative for Germany, as it is called in English, but the *D* is *Deutschland* in German."

Bazyli wasn't sure how much German Ace knew, or even how much of the history of the country he knew. He continued in English, saying the AfD was now the third-largest party in Germany.

"Ace, the classic picture of a neo-Nazi is rare. Today, they do not have shaved heads or bodies covered with tattoos. Rather, they are citizens concerned about the direction of their country and who attend neo-Nazi rallies. Many have elements of the original Nazi beliefs, such as racism, nationalism, anti-Semitism, and Holocaust denial. What is good news is that Sonora's husband, the Count, always supported us. We are optimistic about getting her support." Bazyli took a long sip of wine. "All that means is that we have to be careful about what we do and who watches us."

Ace listened to Bazyli. He wasn't familiar with Austrian politics but knew something about Germany and the AfD. He had learned in operations with the US military in the Middle East that different cultures, politics, and religion put pressure on people to get out. Belief that a better life existed elsewhere was the common thread for immigrants. How difficult their new life could be in western Europe wasn't something they contemplated. To prove to Bazyli that he was one of them, he needed to concentrate on hating immigrants. No matter how hard that would be, supporting ethnic purity would be worse.

Bazyli drained his glass. "Mr. Prowers—"

Ace interrupted him by saying, "Everyone calls me Ace, although no one is sure why. Alfred is my real name, but my grandfather's name was Alfred. When I hear it, I look around for him."

Bazyli smiled. "Okay. Ace it is. Marton has vouched for you. This facility is for training, and you have a strong background in training as well as in planning and computer technology. You may be able to help out in some of our weaker areas."

He opened a box of cigars. Marton accepted one, but Sig and Ace did not. Smoking and being in shape were not compatible.

"Right now, we have a project: the Nazi gold. Without it, the new neo-Nazi groups will have a harder time organizing. Count Lliessle and Marton's father, who worked for him, might have known where it was hidden. They helped transport gold to Argentina in the last years of the war—and into the 1950s. That worked until the dictator Juan Perón died. I know because my father followed the gold until the day he died. He had his own Nazi contacts."

Bazyli continued, "Many Nazi officials had personal accounts in Switzerland. After the fall of Stalingrad, most military men knew the war was lost. That gave them a year or more to set up private accounts in Swiss banks. Next, there is the gold melted into bars from the concentration camp victims. That is the real problem because no one, and I stress *no one*, knows how much gold that is."

He puffed several times on the cigar, deciding to share with Ace some of his childhood memories. It was a way to get Ace to trust him.

"Ace, when I was young, my father took me to a smelting operation in Poland. Bars of gold were in a storage barn. I never forgot how they gleamed in the semidarkness. I know gold is still here. The end of the war was chaos, everyone running in every direction. Trying to dodge the Russians. My hope is that the gold has not been lost forever."

Ace got the point. "We gotta find the gold."

"Yes, and that gold will be used to fund neo-Nazis, right-wingers' intent on forming a Fourth Reich."

Bazyli went on to say that he had no interest in a Fourth Reich, especially after the mess the Third Reich made of the world. Gold gave groups power. He wanted to support that group, whatever, whoever, it might be.

"We answer every request the right-wingers have. I would like to call them new Nazis, but that inflames people. We believe that we are a superior people. Your background fits our profile. Welcome to the cause. I am sure we can benefit from your expertise. Sig will set you up for training. I will tell him not to beat you into the ground with physical exercises."

He laughed, and Ace wondered what he had gotten himself into.

CHAPTER TWENTY-SEVEN

At the Training Facility

Marton and Ace left the mansion and headed down a dirt lane winding through trees. They could see a large running track with several buildings behind it.

"It is Sig," said Marton. "I do not know him that well, but he is in charge of Bazyli's training."

With that, Marton left Ace on his own and headed back to the main house. Sig looked at Ace, obviously sizing him up. Ace knew he was overweight. All Bazyli's men were trim and lean. At least he was taller than most of them. Only Sig, tall and blond, was his height, if not an inch or so taller.

"I read your file and saw that you are an expert on planning and the use of the computer. You can make a contribution to our teams in those areas. We are not as advanced as we would like to be. Let me show you the operations room."

"I'll do my best," said Ace.

Working on technical operations and using the computer were his strengths. Without commenting on Ace's physical shape, Sig told him that the technical area needed to be developed. Ace knew he could handle that and told Sig that information on the web could be useful for operations. He accurately surmised Sig and Bazyli had no idea what could be found.

On the drive from the main part of the mansion, he had seen part of an antenna system in the back of the running track. It could be monitoring cell phones. He still had his phone, as no one had asked him for it. That showed him there were some gaps in security. Now, he needed to look squeaky clean, so he wouldn't use it.

Ace looked around the operations room that Sig said was used for technical intelligence. There were three computers. That was the extent of the group's technical operations. He had his work cut out for him. Sig said the men were not allowed personal computers, though they did have cell phones.

"Now, for the physical fitness," said Sig.

They walked out the back of the townhouses to a track. Ace knew that Bazyli's guys would be testing him. After all, their lives might depend on how reliable he was. By his count, there were at least twenty men, and he estimated that all but three or four were under thirty years old.

Sig announced the required times for laps around the track. Ace managed to run a couple of laps around the track, but his knees told him that was enough. He vowed to walk at least five miles a day.

The men Bazyli had hired were physically fit and not into the mental aspects of what Bazyli might have had in mind for jobs.

I just have to keep ahead of them, he thought.

As he checked his shoelaces, he heard a whistle blow. All the guys headed to the end of the field, where Ace could see that a shooting range was set up. Time for weapons practice. This was something he could excel at. And he did.

About an hour later, Sig came over to him. "Ace, I doubt you need any practice. Every gun and rifle you have fired has been on the bull's-eye. Have you been practicing?"

"I confess," said Ace, "I make it a point to shoot at a range every few months. I enjoy shooting and never know when it will come in handy."

Ace and Sig returned to the computer room. To Ace's surprise, Bazyli's computer system didn't have a central server. Each of the three computers operated independently. It looked like Sig had bought them, one at a time, from a Vienna computer store or online.

In less than an hour, he had prepared a summary of news reports from Europe. Next, he prepared an assessment of where the team would be most effective in disrupting local authorities.

Ace thought, *How easy this is for me.*

The major problem was to figure out how to research the files on all three computers without being caught. It was possible that each had separate files. Most of Sig's team usually worked on the same machine if it was available.

Was it too early to scan this one?

From his years in the government, he knew that there were programs to crack secure accounts and break into password-protected files. But these computers didn't need a sophisticated program to check.

Looking around, though he was alone in the room, he pulled a thumb drive from his pocket and began to copy all the files on the hard drive. Minutes later, he had the data.

Then, he realized, *why copy? All I need to do is find out where the teams are going.*

He'd be in there every day and could monitor the trips on the hard drives that were accessible to everyone.

There was a knock on the door, and Marton entered. "Time for dinner. Bazyli asked me to stay over. He knows Pedro and I are friends, and he likes to talk about his sons with an audience. We need a minute alone from prying eyes." He handed Ace a burner phone. "You need to be able to contact your aunt and Amy. So, here is a way. This burner is the safest. No phone calls on any other phone, Ace."

Ace wondered if this was Sonora's or Marton's idea. It didn't matter; he had what he needed. "Thanks. This will keep Sig from asking questions. I'm sure they trace the calls out of the house. I don't want him to doubt my commitment to their cause. These guys don't let you into the inner circle until you have proven yourself in battle, so to speak."

Ace knew it was important that Sig would think he was loyal, as he was still on probation. "The worry is, how can I get through the security monitors to the dining room and to the gym?"

Marton had to laugh. "They do not have security monitors. The teams carry weapons and their personal cell phones. So, no electronic systems. They would be going off all the time."

"You head over to dinner. I'll meet you there," said Ace. When he prepared the agendas for the teams in the operations room, he had searched the hard drives. Rarely was anyone in the room with him. Now, with everyone at lunch, no one was in the room with him. He could read German better than he could speak it, so his searches didn't take long.

On the last computer he tried, he found what he needed: a reservation for a house in Sylt. The date was in three days for three rooms. What he found odd was that there was no end date. The time was open. He knew he had to call Amy.

"About time I heard from you," she said.

Amy told him that she and Thoren were driving, not flying, to Neustrelitz. She explained that the plane couldn't land at small airports. They would get to Husum late that evening.

"How are you doing finding the gold?" she asked.

"It's been tough. Remember, I have to be part of the group. Fortunately, Amy, I have the right skills. At the moment, I'm alone, but that doesn't happen often. Listen, Amy, Bazyli's guys are staying at a rented house in Husum. Sounds perfect for them. Their stay starts tomorrow. Keep a lookout for them."

"Thanks for the tip, Ace. Stay in touch. None of this is easy, and I wish you were up here with us."

"Hang tight. I may get sent up there. Right now, I'm just monitoring the computers and preparing the day's agendas. You should be able to text me on this phone. Stay in touch. Let me know when you spot these guys. Shouldn't be too hard."

Sarcastically, Amy asked if they wore matching T-shirts.

"No, but look at their waistbands or under their vests. You should be able to see guns."

Again, Amy said she wished he was coming with them, but she knew he had work to do in Vienna. Bob Morris's instinct to send him to work for Bazyli had been right.

CHAPTER TWENTY-EIGHT

In Hohenlychen

Amy looked out the window at the north German countryside and was relieved they had not flown. Flying by private jet was Sonora's idea of efficient travel. Amy had refrained from saying, "Only if you can afford it." She was just as happy to have Thoren drive and to see the countryside up close.

She had to put Ace's phone call aside for now. The scenery was beautiful. Amy felt transported back to how the land must have looked centuries ago. Rivers, fields, forests, and marshland covered the flat ground. Some of the waterways had to be canals. The Germans were famous for connecting natural waterways with canals.

For a moment, she wished all three of her husbands, not just Vince, were here to enjoy the search. At least the last two died without leaving a quest for her. Would she find the Nazi gold that had been so elusive to Vince? She didn't know.

It wasn't the money. Vince believed that the gold represented the lives of the souls who died in World War II. Even if she didn't find it, that she had tried would close this chapter in Vince's life. She looked at Thoren, who was reading a map in his right hand while he drove.

The trip to Husum was just under three hundred miles, a comfortable day's drive from Berlin. Sonora had made reservations at an upscale hotel she knew would please Amy. They would arrive late in the evening because of their stops along the way.

"Okay, Thoren, give me the rundown on Hohenlychen. I know Sonora seemed to think it's worth a stop. She said it's a nice break and about fifty miles from Berlin."

She listened to Thoren, who said that in 1902, the facility was a TB sanatorium under the German Red Cross. In 1935, a Nazi doctor named Karl Gebhardt turned Hohenlychen into a world-class facility, an orthopedic hospital for Nazi elite. He was the surgeon for the SS and the Reich Police—and Himmler's personal physician and childhood friend. Both Himmler and Rudolf Hess lived at the facility for months on end. Himmler's mistress had their two children here.

As Amy listened, she thought, *As psychotic as those two Nazis were, they needed some treatment and rest.*

She wondered aloud what had happened to the children of Nazis.

"Many changed their names. Rarely do they say anything in public or condemn anyone. I am a part of their generation, and Amy, we just want to get on with our lives today. The past is gone, except for this gold issue, which no one can forget. Gold does that to people."

He paused for a moment. "My brother, Frederic, never seemed to get over the war, even though he was born during it. One of the things that General Karl Gebhardt did was experiment on the women who were prisoners at Ravensbrück, a women's concentration camp. It became well known for his experiments on seventy-two Catholic Polish women, who were called the Rabbits of Ravensbrück. It is important because many people think only Jews were in concentration camps. The Jews were the majority, but many other dissidents were also killed in the camps."

That rang a bell with Amy. "I read a book about the Rabbits. I thought the name Ravensbrück sounded familiar. Imagine, Thoren, doing experiments on these prisoners. They named them Rabbits because the women were treated like lab animals. The experiments often left them with injuries that had them hop like rabbits when they walked—at least, the ones who lived."

Thoren said that Ravensbrück was west and a little out of their way. It was on many tours for overseas visitors. Hohenlychen was usually ignored.

"Amy, the buildings for both camps are similar. Ravensbrück has been renovated a little because of the tourists. The idea of it being a women's camp makes it more popular to visit than the hospital at Hohenlychen. What they have in common is that General Gebhardt was the medical doctor for both. He lived in both camps."

Thoren went on, "Himmler realized that the Nazis' days were coming to an end. Using the Swedish Red Cross as a go-between, Himmler tried to broker a truce and surrender. Hohenlychen was evacuated before any agreement was signed, and Himmler killed himself. Within ten days, the Russians had taken the facility. They used it as a military barracks and a hospital until 1993. Since that time, it has been vacant." He added, "Amy, you will see what Hohenlychen was, but nothing is functional today."

She flipped a page in her guidebook. "I see that General Gebhardt was hanged in 1947 for war crimes. Himmler took a cyanide tablet when he was captured. Seems fitting. I mean, he was the man who got rid of opposition to Hitler, ran the police force in the Third Reich, and created the death camps and slave labor camps in eastern Europe. Interesting that he hoped to join the British to fight the Russians. Hitler turned on him, and Himmler tried to escape Germany dressed like an ordinary soldier. Unbelievable, the ego of these guys. They had to be sick."

Amy continued, "I've been to Auschwitz-Birkenau in Poland. The camps make you feel as if you have a hollow space inside. It's hard to describe. The Holocaust museums are where you get a real education. The one in Washington, D.C., is the granddaddy of all Holocaust museums."

Thoren tried to focus on today. He hesitated. "Amy, there is a man in Neustrelitz, a Heidrich Lange, who was a friend of Frederic's. We should talk to him. If we make a brief visit to Hohenlychen and skip Ravensbrück, it will look to him like we are genuine tourists. You the tourist, me the guide. I think we can find him because he still owns a bar in town."

Now, Amy understood. "I get it. We look like tourists, but our goal is to find out what Frederic was doing when he visited Neustrelitz, right?"

"You got it."

"I understand. My aunt coached you."

They both saw the sign for Hohenlychen, which was almost hidden in the hedges, and Thoren took the turn. Immediately, buildings loomed out of a forested area. The silence, eerie and calm, overtook both of them.

The parking lot was empty. Looking around, they saw evidence of construction on some of the large redbrick-and-stone buildings, but it would take years to renovate them all. Covered with vines, windows broken or blackened over, the buildings showed their history. The trees, birds, and small animals knew the stories, but they, too, were silent. Only an odd woodpecker could be heard.

Walking around the still-impressive buildings, they discussed why the German government had not developed the land.

"Maybe Mr. Lang in Neustrelitz will know."

Without a backward glance, they both returned to the car, still feeling the silence. Amy turned one last time to look at the facility. The people were gone. Only the brick-stucco buildings and the ghosts remained.

CHAPTER TWENTY-NINE

Neustrelitz

Neustrelitz was a beautiful little town in the style of seventeenth-century baroque architecture, with white-stucco buildings and red-tile roofs. Located in the middle of the Müritz National Park, it was known as the land of a thousand lakes. Amy noticed that the guidebook said that there were about a hundred lakes.

"Sounds like the perfect place to have lunch," she said. And it was.

The streets in the center were arranged like spokes in a wheel, but Thoren zipped through it. He knew the area. "We used to stop here for lunch when we went to Husum. The castle was bombed in World War II, and all that is left is a nice garden.

We will meet Heidrich Lange at a café on the lake called the Zierker See. The Fisherhof on the lake is the best place to eat."

Thoren added, "In case you are wondering, Sonora set this up. I do not know this Lange, but she does. Seems he knew Frederic, as his son and Frederic were good friends. That means he has to be an old Communist who lived here during the Russian occupation. That is not the worst of his history. Sonora told me he was a Nazi. We will not mention that."

Amy understood. Today, no one ever admitted to being a Nazi.

"I read somewhere that this area of Mecklenburg province is a breeding ground for the neo-Nazi movement, or whatever the right-wingers call themselves."

"Yes," said Thoren. "Oh, Amy, do not ask about his son. He was killed in an accident just before Frederic left for South Africa."

"How does Sonora know him?" she asked.

"Probably from her husband or from Frederic. She and my brother were very close."

Amy tucked that information away. Sonora had told her that Frederic seemed to know everyone and that everyone knew him.

As they arrived at the restaurant, Amy could see fishermen unloading fresh fish from a boat. At least the meal would be good. An outdoor patio opened onto the lakeshore. She felt a sense of peace. It was such a perfect view.

An elderly, balding man stood up and waved to them. He introduced himself in English as Heidrich Lange, and he said to call him Henry.

"Is it just the two of you?" They nodded. "Sorry, figured Bazyli would have you followed."

"Maybe he did," said Amy, "but we didn't notice anyone."

Henry smiled, knowing Bazyli's boys would never be seen.

"This is the place to eat fish." The waiter brought a bottle of white wine, and Henry indicated to bring one more. "This has been my restaurant for fifty years. Herring is the number one fish for Germans, but the cod and the perch are also good. The bays of the Baltic Sea mix with the freshwater rivers of Germany and support freshwater fish. If you like fish, you will enjoy this meal."

"White wine goes with fish, right?"

They laughed.

Amy said, "I'll drink any wine with fish."

Henry laughed, and Amy found herself liking him.

Then, she realized, *If he had been a spy in the days when the area was in East Germany, that was what they did: got you to like them and to trust them.*

Thoren said they couldn't spend all afternoon, as they had to get to Husum that night. Henry said it shouldn't be a problem; the roads were good, and they would arrive in Husum just after dinner. Since dinner was usually at nine o'clock, Thoren wasn't thrilled. But it was easy enough to do.

By the second glass of wine, and halfway through the wonderful fresh perch that Henry recommended, their host came to the point. "You must be looking for the gold that Frederic hid, right? I mean, everyone comes here to find it. Oh, and to enjoy the fish."

They nodded.

"It is not here. Before he left for South Africa, if he ever did leave, he came by and took it. North, I think. He had three trucks and stayed at my house that night."

He went on to say he had helped because his son, before he died, had asked him to assist Frederic. "I did it for my son; it is that simple."

"Do you have any idea where in the north he took it?" asked Amy.

"Not really. Could be in Denmark or Norway. I don't know."

For a moment, they sipped their wine. It was time to go, but Henry had another question. "Where is Frederic? Is he dead like so many seem to think?"

"I do not know," said Thoren. "My mother thinks he is alive. She says her heart tells her so."

"She is not alone in thinking that. So does Bazyli Czartoryski," said Henry. "I spoke to him after I heard his son Uwe was killed in Nuremberg."

"My cousin and I were there when it happened," said Amy. She felt it was wise to say they had been there. It was very likely that Henry already knew that. If he didn't, then it couldn't hurt to say so.

"Terrible thing to lose your son." And with that, Thoren stood up. "We really have to go, Henry. Thanks for lunch, and stay in touch. If we find the gold, we will let you know."

They shook hands, and as they left, Amy looked at the peaceful lake. Somehow, the tranquility she thought it had when they arrived was gone.

Henry watched them go and reached for his cell phone. Simon Bell was waiting for his call. All he could tell his friend was that the two were heading north. They were going to Frederic's house in Husum, but why? Everyone involved knew that Frederic, with the help of the monks, had moved the gold south.

Before he could dial the number, the waiter was at his side. "You were right, boss. They were followed. A man is now walking down to the lake on a little-used path. He doesn't know they left, and he doesn't know the area."

To Henry, it made sense that Bazyli, the old Russian, would have Amy followed. "Take the guy out. Strangers who do not know the currents drown all the time."

• • •

Horst knew he was late, having missed the turn, but Amy and Thoren were still on the outdoor patio, eating. In this part of Mecklenburg, the roads were tricky and went in all directions. Raised in this part of the province, he knew the restaurant where they would probably be eating and quickly found them.

He took a fishing rod and a long rifle from the backseat and headed for the lake. But as he walked between the boathouses to the lake, he saw them leave. Their lunch had been short, and he wasn't set up. At least he could kill Heidrich, the old Nazi. That would please Bazyli.

Crossing behind one of the boathouses, he headed for the small pier on the lake. From there, he would have a view of the entire restaurant and pick Heidrich off. But again, he was too late.

An arm encircled his throat, and he was unconscious in a minute. Two of Heidrich's men hauled him into a small rowboat and headed out to the center of the lake. The body should wash up on the shore or, with good luck, be carried out to sea.

CHAPTER THIRTY

In Husum

The next morning, looking out the dining room window of the Theodor Storm Hotel, Amy imagined how the harbor at Husum looked decades ago. A beach town for centuries and a one-time port, Husum today seemed as if its heyday had passed. The streets were clean, and the buildings looked like they did in the nineteenth century. Had the town always been so quiet?

The rolls were homemade, and the coffee was delicious. Sonora was right—no stars but up to international standards.

"Thoren, what did this town look like when your brother bought his house?"

"He did not buy it. His wife's family has owned it for a century," said Thoren. "Frederic and his wife would have moved to

Spain because they loved the beaches, but this house was a gift from his wife's family. She was the only heir to some German Count who had property up here. After his wife died, Frederic lived here year-round. Said he loved the memories. The view from the house is of the mudflats, but it is always changing with the tides and bird migrations."

"Pardon me, I heard your conversation," interrupted the hotel manager, who introduced himself as Klaus Meyer and a friend of Sonora Lliessle's and of Thoren's brother, Frederic.

Klaus didn't have to ask who Thoren was. Of medium height, with light-blond, almost brown, hair, he was so physically fit one would say he was thin. Thoren, like Frederic, could be a native of any country in western Europe.

"The real beaches are just north of here on Sylt Island. White sands and blue seas as long as the sky is clear."

"I read that's where the rich live—or, I should say, where the rich vacation," said Amy.

Looking at Klaus, she thought he was about Sonora's age. He was tall, with perfect Aryan features, and she could see he must have looked like a poster boy for the Nazis when he was young. Today, he was overweight, with very gray hair. He was taller than Ace; she guessed his height at six feet eight.

What, she wondered, *is he doing in Husum? Is he really retired?*

Isolated in northern Germany on the coast, Husum seemed to be a place for retired spies.

Klaus leaned his long body over the table, poured more coffee in each cup, and proceeded to educate them on the islands. "Sylt Island is the largest island in a chain of islands we call the North Frisian Islands. Today, the society folks from Hamburg spend weekends in their fancy houses and eat at the elite restaurants. During World War II, the entire island was a military base.

"Houses on the beach have the best views of the seacoast, but they are not protected from the storms that roll in off the sea. In the old days, there were floods, and the mudflats protected the houses on the flats, like Frederic's. Farther north on the island, there is no protection from the sea. Some of the houses have retaining walls, but they block the view of the ocean, and who can say if they really work. Only the Germans who consider themselves elite stay up there."

He smiled. "That is why we like it here in Husum. We just muddle along and do not have to worry about who is who, or whom. We know the best dish to eat is a fresh fish sandwich."

Thoren told him that since Frederic's house had been closed for several years, they had decided to stay at the hotel. Klaus said he had a set of keys to Frederic's house because he looked after it for him. Thoren was pleased to hear about the keys, but it was news to him. How like Frederic to make his own arrangements in private.

"This evening, after dinner, I will serve you our coastal coffee—rum in coffee, topped with cream. It is called a *Pharisäer*, as in the Pharisees."

"What a name," said Amy.

Klaus laughed. "It started when the locals used the cream to hide the smell of alcohol from the clergymen. But the clergy caught on and called them Pharisees. The name stuck."

Amy asked him why the name of the hotel was the same name as that of nineteenth-century writer Theodor Storm.

Klaus smiled. "I am impressed that you know about him. Storm is considered to be one of the most important nineteenth-century German realists. He did his work in that century, but he became popular again in the twentieth century. His house is now a small museum—and an interesting place to visit."

"I didn't know that," said Amy. "I knew that the final of his, I think, fifty novellas, *The Rider on the White Horse*, is said to be his masterpiece. While a little depressing, he keeps you reading. What really gets me is that the plot and ending stay with you. I knew the setting was the northern German coast; I just didn't realize it was this piece of coastal land."

Klaus laughed and said, "It is here, all right. His last novella, which describes the North Frisian Islands, the mudflats, the fog, the wild winds, is famous as a battleground, man versus nature, the dikes and the sea. Amy, if you have read his work, you understand these islands."

They needed to see Frederic's house, and they told Klaus they would be back for dinner. He noted that the hotel's microbrewery would be open in the late afternoon.

"Sometimes, right-wing extremists populate my bar. I will make sure they do not bother you."

"We will be back early," said Thoren.

Amy quickly agreed. The bar sounded more interesting than the house.

Klaus watched them go, again thinking he would have known Thoren anywhere. He was the spitting image of Frederic.

• • •

The road angled along the bay beside rows of beach houses that Amy thought looked at least a hundred years old. They were stucco, so she knew they would hold up against the north winds. Frederic's house was no different, just bigger. Beside it was a small graveyard.

"Here in northern Germany, there are many stories of grave robbers, but none have found their way to this family plot—at least so far." Thoren explained that his brother's wife had a large family who often visited, and many chose to be buried in the graveyard.

As they pulled into the driveway, two motorcycles zoomed by, quickly moving down the road and out of sight.

"Are we being followed, or am I paranoid?" said Amy.

Ace had warned her that some of Bazyli's men had reservations in Husum. She had kept it to herself. No point in making Thoren paranoid about being followed. She would like to have told Klaus, but she didn't know him. Besides, whose side was he on?

They both knew it was possible that right-wing extremists were watching the house. Klaus had said that some members were in town—or at least drinking in his bar. She wished he had called them neo-Nazis.

"Thoren, what is that?" She pointed to what looked like a piece of wood sticking up not far from shore.

"That is the gear for the rollers to move the dredge in and out of the water. With climate change and water usage high in cities like Hamburg, the water level is lower. Years ago, you would never have seen the top of the platform."

She asked, "Why a dredge? Were they digging a channel for larger ships?"

To her, it was a joke, but Thoren said, "Or submarines."

"Seriously, Thoren. Now, we're getting somewhere. My guidebook said that this bay is a large mudflat. A dredge could dig a channel for any ship. What's that odd-shaped building next to the main house? A boathouse?"

"Yes, it stores the dredge. Let us take a look at it."

The padlock on the door opened easily using one of the keys on the chain. Amy realized that Klaus was doing his job as caretaker for the property.

They stepped inside and saw that the dredge filled the boathouse. It was on rollers connected to a cable and a lift for digging out silt. Some parts of it were old because they were wooden, yet all the metal parts glistened as if they had been polished today. They both thought the same thing; someone had either used the dredge or kept it available for use.

"Is it true that dredges have a barge beside them that they can put the dirt, the silt, on?"

Thoren shrugged and said that the barge could have sunk in the bay where the wooden stake was. He looked at her.

"Are you thinking that the gold could be on the barge?"

"Exactly."

Amy repeated what Klaus had said the night before: that everyone had combed the property looking for the gold and found nothing. He'd told them right-wing groups had traveled to Husum and searched for the gold.

She paused. "It's very likely that they looked in the bay, but why would your brother keep the house and the dredge in working condition and not use it? Someone else kept it in working order. The barge holding the gold could be sunk in the bay in front of us, and no one would be the wiser."

Thoren looked again at the dredge. "To start, the dredge takes a generator. The power is off in the house. Maybe Klaus can help us."

CHAPTER THIRTY-ONE

At the Beach House

The train trip to Husum was a testimony to the picturesque northern German towns. Sig thought this part of Germany would be less populated and was surprised to see more houses. More people meant that his team, Raul and Peter, would be less conspicuous.

Bazyli had insisted that he would lead the team. One team was monitoring the Lliessle villas in Zurich. The men with him in Husum were untested and needed supervision. Bazyli trusted him because they both knew that gold bars were a temptation for many men.

So, I am here, he thought.

He still hoped that they might get in some fishing. The rods and reels were packed in their luggage so that they could fish out on the western edge of the mudflats. He knew the tides brought in an array of fish. His favorite was always North Sea sole. And the oysters. The more he thought about it, the more he realized the trip was worth it just to have fresh oysters.

The train pulled to a stop in the small station at Husum. In the parking lot, Sig could see the rental SUV.

"Okay, boss. Where are we staying?" asked Raul.

"At a private house. Big hotels are not the right fit for what we are doing. Soon as we settle in, we will head to the Theodor Storm Hotel, where Amy and Thoren are staying. The hotel has an excellent bar and restaurant that is popular with the locals. We should fit right in. I texted Horst our address. Not sure why he has not showed up. Not like him."

With the car's GPS, they were at the house in ten minutes. To Sig, the house was perfect. Located on one of the least-occupied stretches of land along the mudflats, it also was just down the road from Frederic's wife's beach house.

• • •

Klaus Meyer didn't expect a call from Simon Bell and was surprised when he called. He was even more surprised to hear why he called.

"Wanted you to know that Amy Prowers and Thoren are looking for the gold that was stored at Frederic's wife's house."

"So they told me." Klaus paused for a moment and then spoke with authority. "They are too late. Frederic moved it. It is gone, but I am not going to tell them. Besides, no one is sure that he moved all of it."

Klaus's gut told him that Frederic had taken all the gold out of Husum when he left five years ago. Problem was, no one was interested in his gut; they wanted evidence.

He went on to say that diving in the mudflats was worthless. All you got was mud. Something as heavy as gold bars would sink into the mud and be lost forever.

"Simon, do you really want to swim around in the mud?"

"No, and I agree that it is very likely that Frederic took all of the gold out and headed south. But don't dissuade Amy and Thoren. Let them do their thing, but keep an eye on them. And Klaus, expect Bazyli to send his guys up there to watch them."

"Are they in danger?"

Simon didn't think so. "But we know when gold is involved, anything can happen."

Klaus agreed and thanked Simon for the call.

Putting the phone down, he looked around the bar. No skinheads so far. But Simon wouldn't have called unless he thought there would be trouble. He unlocked a cabinet under the bar and took out two pistols. If Bazyli's crowd was coming, then he couldn't be too careful.

• • •

Amy sat in the bar at the Theodor Storm Hotel, feeling very comfortable. A beer and some of Klaus's cook's wonderful bratwurst had done wonders for her. Thoren had gone to the bank. The money left in the accounts would go to his mother, but what was in the safe-deposit box?

She had barely finished her bratwurst when he was back. "Empty."

"Empty," she repeated.

"Whatever was in the safe-deposit box is gone, and it was a large box," said Thoren. "The bank accounts showed the same deposit as before, and my name and our mother's name were on the account."

Amy was glad that Thoren and his mother would get the money. But what could have been in the safe-deposit box?

"Thoren, have you or your mother talked to Frederic's company in South Africa?"

"*Ja*, they say he is on a special assignment, only what is odd is they cannot tell you where he is. That and my mother's intuition is why she says he is still alive. I did not think he was a spook, but maybe he is."

Amy nodded but was really thinking about how gold changed people. It sounded like it had changed Frederic. But that wasn't any help in figuring out where he was. Right now, to find the gold, if it was in the mudflats, then they needed a generator to power the motor on the dredge.

Klaus stood at the door to the bar, and she waved him over to her table. They asked him about the generator. Thoren explained that they needed it to operate the dredge and to pull up the platform.

"I have an extra one in our warehouse."

She and Thoren thanked him.

Klaus smiled. "I knew there was a platform, some type of barge, in the mudflats. With Hamburg taking our water, the level has really gone down. Been thinking it might surface one of these days. Sometimes, we could see bits of it. Never thought it was connected to the gold."

Amy told him that both she and Thoren thought that the barge might be where the gold was stored. Klaus was not so sure. He said that the flats had been searched by boat several times just in the three years he had lived in Husum.

Klaus wished them good luck. "Enjoy your drinks. Oh, you may run into an elderly couple who live next door to Frederic's house. They often walk along the road. They know everything that happens out that way, are friendly, and might be able to help you."

After he left, Thoren said, "We have the generator, and to-morrow, we should find out if the barge is in the mudflats."

"Yes," said Amy, and she reached into her jacket pocket for her vibrating cell phone. She answered and heard Bob Morris's voice.

"Your aunt called me in Zurich. She wanted me to touch base with you and see if anything of interest has come up in Denmark."

Amy said, "Nothing so far. Bob, you know we're in Germany."

"Yes, but you're so far north you may as well be in Denmark. Have you seen any minders? You know what they are?"

"Spooks monitoring spooks. Only, we aren't spooks."

"I know, but some of the radical right-wingers might be up there. If something unusual comes up, give me a call. See you back in Zurich very soon. Goodbye."

Amy looked at Thoren. "Bob Morris thinks we should be back in Zurich."

Thoren shrugged. "Who knows? Now let us, eat, drink, and relax."

• • •

Sig parked the SUV around the corner from the Theodor Storm Hotel. The entrance to the bar was a few yards away. They were hungry and ready for a cold beer.

The pub was inside the hotel in a separate room and filled with what Sig thought were more locals than tourists. Some even had shaved heads. He was relieved that his guys wouldn't look out of place. Bazyli had told him that the northern states were right wing, and he was right. He knew the AfD Party was strong in the north.

The waiter brought the menu, and Sig waved him away. "We are here for your fish. What is your best entrée?"

"Fish and chips."

Sig looked at his team. They nodded.

"And I hope you have some fresh oysters?"

The waiter smiled. "Always. And beer?"

"Large mugs, please," said Sig.

None of the other patrons paid any attention to them. They were seated in the back of the room and had a good view. Amy and Thoren weren't in the pub.

"Boss," said Peter, "this is a good gig. Eating and drinking."

"Right, give me a minute," said Sig. "I want to check out the hotel, maybe pick up some brochures."

The lobby wasn't large and had a table of pamphlets and information on what to do in Husum, from tours to boating. As he flipped through the pamphlets, the elevator door opened, and Amy Prowers and Thoren stepped out. He recognized them from Bazyli's pictures. They headed into the bar.

Perfect, thought Sig.

"Can I help you?" Klaus had seen a man looking at the brochures and knew he wasn't a local.

"Just passing through. Taking some brochures in case I come back again. Interested in fishing."

"Our fishing is great, and here is my card. Don't hesitate to give me a call if you need reservations. We can also arrange a boat."

Sig thanked him and went back to the bar.

Klaus waited for a moment and followed him into the bar, going behind the counter and pulling out some paperwork. From there, he could view the entire bar. He noted that the man joined two other men with shaved heads. Not unusual up here in Husum. Then, he saw Amy and Thoren sitting at a table in the middle of the room.

Interesting coincidence, he thought. *Why are they all here together?*

The next morning, Amy and Thoren took the generator and followed the sea of mudflats up the road to Frederic's house. As they pulled up to the gate, Amy noticed an SUV parked about a half mile up the road. What was it doing? Looking out on the bay, she could see no houses south along the mudflats. All she could see was empty water. She shook her head. Ace's phone call was making her see Bazyli's men everywhere.

But then, she thought, *Maybe they are everywhere.*

Thoren opened the gate lock and pulled into the circular driveway. He went in the boathouse door and proceeded to hook up the generator. Amy watched as he attached the pump, which fit perfectly into the side of the dredge. He found the outlet for the hook in the dredge.

"Now, let us see if it works," he said. He flipped the switch and the generator sputtered, then started. As it did, he flipped the switch on the side of the dredge, and its motor started. "Magic." He grinned. "I do not know if they have been used since Frederic was here. What was that, oh, five years ago?"

"I am impressed," said Amy.

"Confession time," said Thoren. "We had a similar dredge pump at a cabin our family owned on a lake when I was a kid. Spent a couple of summers there and learned from my father. Obviously, Frederic remembered how to use it."

He reached around and turned another switch. The pulley began to wind up the cable. They both watched the water in the mudflats, and after a minute, the platform started to emerge. It was the flat base. Nothing was on top of it.

Silently, they stared at the platform. Amy finally spoke. "Could the gold have fallen off into the mudflats?"

"No, I do not think so. That would be unusual, and if it did, we would never find it. The gold would sink through the mud to the middle of the earth."

"Oh, pardon." They whirled around at the sound of the voice to see an elderly couple wearing walking shoes and carrying walking sticks. They were dressed in heavy woolen jackets and pants, and Amy was sure the clothes were left over from the world war. "We saw you working with the dredge. Are you looking for the gold?"

Without thinking, both Amy and Thoren said yes. This elderly couple hardly looked like gold thieves. They could barely walk.

"It has been gone for some time. Was supposed to be a secret that Frederic brought it here just before his wife died. Years later, he took it away, then brought it back. No wonder folks are confused as to where it is. Many people have searched the bay and the graveyard, but nothing has been found."

Amy and Thoren were silent for a moment, then Amy recovered her voice. "You know if there is anything left on the submerged barge?"

They were silent.

"Thoren, you know my ability to speak German sucks. Could you ask them what they know about the barge?"

She listened to Thoren, following most of the conversation. Why was it so easy to understand German but so hard to speak it?

What the old man had to say was almost unbelievable. He told them that monks came in two large trucks and helped Frederic load the boxes off the barge. Then, they drove away. He didn't know where they were going but was sure it was south, like Berlin.

What he said next was a surprise. "The monks and Frederic came back three more times. Each time with at least three vans. I think there was more than one platform in the mudflats."

Thoren asked him if they got everything out of the mudflats.

"*Ja*, Frederic himself told me they were finished. He said he would be back in the fall to visit, but that was the last time we saw him. He said he would be out of the country for some time." He looked at his wife, who nodded.

The man had spoken in halting English, which was the only reason Amy could understand him.

"If anything was left on it, it is sunk to the middle of the earth. The past few years, we had some big storms. No barge could survive."

"And," asked Amy, "do you remember how many years ago you saw him?"

"Oh." He looked at his wife. "Was it five years ago?"

"Yes." The woman was positive. "I remember because we just bought our new motor for our rowboat, and Frederic helped us figure out how to operate it. The manuals they include are useless."

"They do not make those manuals readable," said the man.

With a nod of their heads, the couple went on hiking along the road toward the last house along the mudflats.

Amy looked down the road for the SUV she had seen parked there, but it was gone.

• • •

Watching in the SUV from the road above the house, Sig knew it was time to go when the old couple started talking to Amy and Thoren. He had also seen the empty platform they had pulled from the water.

"We are leaving. The gold is gone. Maybe we can fish in the morning and take the noon train back to Hamburg. From there, we fly back to Vienna. Will have to hope that Horst heads back to Vienna, if he shows up at all."

"Works for us, boss," said his team in unison.

• • •

The street in front of the Theodor Storm Hotel was dark and slightly damp, as if it had rained. Amy and Thoren realized that it was too late to drive back to Berlin that night, especially if there was a storm.

"How about we leave at five in the morning? Should take about four hours if we go directly to Berlin. Last time, we went east, so it took longer," said Thoren.

Amy agreed. Now, looking around the bar at the hotel, she realized that they had spent more time in it than anywhere else. Their beer had just arrived when the manager, Klaus, joined them.

"Neither of you look jubilant, like you found anything."

Was there any harm in telling Klaus? Amy didn't think so and proceeded to give him an update.

"Monks. That is odd," said Klaus. "Frederic was here before my time. I have been here only three years. Still, would have thought someone would have seen them."

"It is an isolated road outside of town," said Thoren. "If they came at night in bad weather, no one would be out that way. Surprised me that the old couple had seen the monks' trucks and heard the word Berlin. But they had the date right. Frederic left Germany very close to five years ago."

Klaus told them that the cook made a stew and fresh strudel for the evening meal. Coffee and rolls would be ready for their early morning departure.

"I hope you will return soon and enjoy better weather. Boating is a real pleasure in the summer."

Both assured him they would. After all, Frederic still owned the house.

Then, Amy asked him if any visitors to Husum looked out of place. Klaus knew she was asking whether any right-wingers had arrived. Amy clarified, "I guess I should say, any visitors who might be looking for the gold."

He paused as if thinking, then said, "Did have some new fellows in here eating and drinking. Three men; they were here when you arrived. Nothing special about them—just my nose telling me to watch them. They left after you did."

Amy told him about the SUV that was sitting at the end of the road. "It seemed to be watching us. But I couldn't see inside—too far away. May be my imagination."

"What happened to it?" asked Klaus.

"It left after we pulled the empty platform out of the water."

Klaus shrugged. "Hard to say what it was doing. But it is odd that it was just sitting on the road next to the mudflats. I mean, there is nothing out there but mud."

"Right. No harm done," said Amy. She sounded positive, but her intuition told her that the vehicle had been watching them.

Their meal arrived, and Klaus watched them for a moment until they settled in to eat. He headed out the back of the hotel to his van. Inside was a burner cell phone.

It took only a moment to place the call to Simon, who he assumed was in Berlin. Klaus didn't have to identify himself; Simon would know who it was from the number.

"Well, my friend, the two you know said nothing was on the platform. But an old couple who live at the end of the road were out walking and saw them pulling up the dredge. According to the old couple, who have lived most of their lives along the flats, monks came in trucks and took away the boxes that the dredge pulled up from the barge. Where they took them, the old couple was not sure, but they thought they heard Berlin."

Simon wanted to know when this happened. Klaus repeated what Amy and Thoren had told him. The couple thought it was about five years ago because that was when they bought their rowboat, and Frederic helped them operate the new motor.

"And Simon, three guys were up here eating at the hotel. They did not look like they were into Theodor Storm novels. Amy thought she saw an SUV watching them at Frederic's house. May have been Bazyli's guys watching them."

"Thank you," said Simon. "I keep hoping one day to get there for some fishing."

"I will be ready," said Klaus, wondering if Simon would ever have time for fishing.

CHAPTER THIRTY-TWO

Outside Vienna

Once Marton left for Berlin, Ace was on his own. The burner phone was on his waist, hidden by the monk's robes. So far, no one had objected that he was wearing monk's robes. In fact, Sig thought his robe was a great cover.

He might not be able to run with Sig's men, but his scores on the firing range had earned him credibility and respect from the members of the organization. Fortunately, he never forgot how to shoot.

It's like riding a bicycle, he thought.

Over the years, when an opportunity came to shoot at a range, he did. He had kept up his expert level on long-range rifles and pistols.

"You are experienced with a gun," said Sig. "Your accuracy on the long rifles will be helpful, but your work on preparing agendas and organizing the teams is the best. And we need it."

"Thanks," said Ace.

The next day, after preparing the agenda for the teams, Ace searched the hard drives. Rarely was anyone in the room with him. He could read German better than he could speak it, so his searches didn't take long. So far, he had found nothing but the reservation in Husum.

. . .

Ace knew when Bazyli invited him to lunch that he must want to discuss something important. He was in his second week, and already, Sig was giving him more work on the computer—and compliments.

They waited, as Sig poured the wine, for Bazyli to take the lead in the discussion.

"Sig tells me that you have become part of the team. Already, you have restructured the training schedule. The men are getting more exercise and more time off. Sig says the drills are more productive. Good work. Now, I want you to know how we began—our philosophy, so to speak. But Ace, do not forget our main goal for now is to find the Nazi gold." He paused and smiled. "And along the way, anything we can do to upset the current political establishment."

He picked up a large book. "A supernatural history of the Nazis, which today hardly anyone mentions. I will read you a paragraph because it tells you how the Nazis manipulated the

German people. I am sure you didn't learn this in your years with the American military. I will paraphrase."

Ace leaned back and listened as Bazyli talked on.

He said many Nazis rejected the Christian idea of good and evil as an Old Testament Jewish invention. To them, what others saw as good was evil, and evil was good. It was called the new morality. Hitler often said that man's spiritual relationship to nature came from ancient gods. From them, he produced his own cult and the pompous rituals, marching around with flags and burning torches. In the nineteenth century, the Germans and the Austrians were consumed studying astrology and parapsychology. This continued into the twentieth century, when over three hundred groups identified with the occult.

"What the groups agreed on was the need for Germany to rise again. This was the emotion that Hitler fed into. The German people, swept along on emotions and on a belief that they had been wronged in the settlement of World War I, let their instincts overrule their intellect.

"Ace, I wanted to share this with you because it is the heart of our movement. This book and others are in my library. Feel free to read them. I give lectures to the men using examples from the histories of the Third Reich, but lately, I have not had time."

"I look forward to reading it," said Ace as the food, chicken on a bed of rice, arrived. Never was he so glad to see chicken.

But not even the food stopped Bazyli.

"Ace, the gold the Nazis confiscated in World War II is still in Germany. The searches in Austria are for ignorant treasure hunters. The right-wingers in Germany were born and raised in what was East Germany, where economic development has been weak, resulting in few jobs. They are eager to find the Nazi gold which they believe is their legacy."

Ace knew that East Germany lagged in development and that this had contributed to the rise of the AfD. "Bazyli, I thought low wages in East Germany contributed to the rise of the right-wingers."

"Exactly," said Bazyli. "Thirty years have passed since 1989 and the fall of the Berlin Wall and the unification of both Germanies. Still, no major German companies are headquartered in the east. Corporations still think of it as Communist territory. The young people migrate to West Germany to work. Now, the pendulum is swinging back a bit."

According to Bazyli, the former East Germany had a low rate of immigration, which helped make it the seat of the AfD's power. "Do not get me wrong, Ace; we are not tied to that group. What we do tends to support their agenda. Our goal is to unite Austria with Germany."

"So," said Ace, "East Germany is still like it was before the immigration of people from the Middle East and from Africa?"

"Right." Bazyli took a long drink out of his wine glass. "Ace, what I need is for you to spread information that supports our politics. It may sound odd, but with your technical background in intelligence, I know you can do it. We are talking about a country that produced Goethe, Beethoven, Bach, Schiller, Einstein, Kant, and Hegel. Yet, in the first half of the last century, over eighty million Germans lost their way following the Third Reich."

Bazyli looked at Ace over his wine glass. "It will not be easy."

Ace felt compelled to say how much he believed that World War I had led to World War II. He knew today that most historians agreed with that fact.

Bazyli listened, stroked his moustache, and continued, "Our movement always needs funds. What gets my goat is that today, Jews—or rather, Israel—will get the gold. You would think the payments made in 1999 and 2000 for reparations would be good enough."

"Payments?" asked Ace.

"Yes, it is complicated."

According to Bazyli, in the Holocaust era, 1933 to 1945, over 6.8 million Swiss bank accounts were opened. When the committees from the United States and Switzerland began in 1999 to investigate bank accounts, over 2.7 million accounts had been destroyed, yet today, there are over 4.1 million Holocaust-era accounts in Swiss banks.

He sighed. "Maybe the Swiss didn't try hard enough to find the heirs—if in some cases, they tried at all."

For once, Ace was glad his mouth was full of sausage, preventing a response. He nodded. He wanted to bring up the fact that the banks required death certificates from the survivors. Only, the concentration camps didn't issue death certificates, which the banks knew. No point in mentioning that. He needed to stay in Bazyli's good graces.

CHAPTER THIRTY-THREE

From Vienna to Zurich

Ace, working on his physical fitness, was on his second lap around the track when he noticed that Sig had disappeared. He could see the path that led into the woods, and he slowly jogged off the track to follow him. The path curved around a low hill. Ahead, he could see Sig weaving in and out of the woods. Below the path was a creek—really a small river. Then, as if he fell in a hole, Sig just disappeared.

Ace stopped peering through the trees. He couldn't see which way Sig had gone. A few minutes passed, and he saw Sig between the branches, standing near the river. Taking cover behind one of the river rocks, he watched Sig head back in the direction of the track. Why was Sig being secretive?

Ace followed the trail to where it ended. He noticed a rock ledge and several boards that looked like they covered an opening. Reaching down, he easily moved them aside and found himself looking at the top of stairs heading down inside a rock wall.

Ace looked around and thought, *why not?* He happened to have a small flashlight, along with matches, a screwdriver, and a pocketknife. He'd learned a long time ago to always be prepared. If only he had a gun. Well, nothing was perfect.

He headed down the stairs and came to the entrance of a cave. The walls of the cave were rocky and damp. His flashlight picked up what looked like a wall. But then, he realized he was looking at stacks of boxes piled up on each other.

Using his knife, he cut a slit in one of the boxes. He turned the flashlight on its contents. The reflection of gold filled the area.

"Bars of gold," he said to himself. "My God . . . Did Bazyli have the Nazi gold all along?"

He tried to walk around the boxes, but the cave was small. Only about ten boxes were stacked against the rock wall.

No, he thought, *this can't be all the Nazi gold.*

But that Bazyli had a few boxes of gold made him wonder if the old man didn't know where the rest of the gold was hidden.

He turned to climb up the stairs and found himself looking at Sig.

"I thought I saw you following me."

"I was jogging and got lost on this trail. Sig, how much gold is down here?"

Sig shrugged. "I do not know the number of bars. You can ask Bazyli. He needs to know you found the cache. Let us go see him."

Bazyli was in his study looking at reports when they arrived. Sig told him that Ace found the cave where the gold was stored.

"He was lost, Bazyli," said Sig. "He tried to jog in the woods, but it was too dense."

Bazyli was surprised, but he trusted Sig. Even more important was that he needed Ace's skills to update his men's training. He and Sig could keep an eye on the Prowers heir.

Opening a bottle of single malt scotch, Bazyli poured three glasses. And then, he surprised Ace, who expected a reprimand.

"No problem, Ace, that you know about the gold. It is not what you think it is. During the war, my family brought the gold, which our family had owned for decades, from Vilnius to Vienna. We acquired more gold for services my family performed, not during World War II but when the Russians ran East Germany. Frederic brought it from Husum."

His huge hands picked up a glittering gold lighter, which Ace knew was gold plated, and lit a cigar. Sig poured more scotch for Ace and himself.

"It is very likely that the gold you saw was once part of *Raubgold*, the stolen Nazi gold that your cousin Amy and Thoren are trying to find. I doubt anyone would understand today that Frederic gave it to me over thirty years ago, when the wall came down between East and West Berlin."

He went on to say that his family had helped the East German government during the years the wall was up. Ace noticed that he didn't say what the Czartoryskis had done to help the East Germans. It didn't seem the right time to ask him. Bazyli was on a roll.

"Frederic always knew where the gold was. I know Amy and Thoren are going to Husum, to Frederic's dead wife's house. I am not sure, but I think at one time, the gold was hidden up there. Frederic was a believer in professional, modern bullion storage facilities. He would have a fit if he saw the gold in the cave. Hiding it in mudflats was also out of character, and that is why he moved it.

"The Swiss have many bullion storage facilities, and it is very likely that Frederic moved the gold into one of those." He poured more scotch. "I am not sure it is hidden in Husum now. Just not sure."

Ace saw an opening. "Is Frederic dead or not?"

Both Bazyli and Sig laughed.

Sig said, "No one is really sure. He left for South Africa, and no one, not even his mother, has heard from him since. His company told his mother he was on assignment, and that was it."

Bazyli was adamant. "What is for sure is that Frederic made the arrangement for my family to get our share and that he has to know where the rest is hidden. Realize, Ace, that what you saw in the cave is just a dribble of the gold that is out there.

"One of our family's long-time employees knew about a smelting plant in Poland. At that plant, the Nazis melted down the gold from the concentration camp prisoners. The melting went on for almost two years. Tell me, how many bars can be made in two years?" He held up his hands. "No one knows."

"Quite right," said Ace. He knew it was important that he appeared loyal. "What I found in the woods on your property is a secret I will keep. I'm on your team, Bazyli. My cousin is determined to find the gold because it was the search her first husband was on when he died. She knows it won't bring him back, but it will close the book on his life. In some way, it will give his death meaning. Even though the way he died had nothing to do with the gold."

"I understand," said Bazyli.

"Bazyli, I will keep you informed on anything my cousin Amy finds."

"Agreed," said Bazyli.

They left Bazyli still drinking scotch. Ace apologized to Sig. "I hope you know I'm not sneaking around. I just got tired of running around the track, and the woods looked inviting. My home is behind the computer, where I am most comfortable."

Sig could see that Ace was overweight and knew he didn't get that way because he exercised. "I know your skills. Your training schedule has already saved our teams valuable man hours. Your strong suit is planning."

"Thank you," said Ace.

He felt that he had justified himself but knew he would have to watch his back. He couldn't afford another gaffe. If he found something on the gold during his computer searches, then he would have to share it with Bazyli. Sharing would prove his loyalty to Bazyli and his men.

Ace returned to the computer room and began a search for bullion facilities in Switzerland. Bazyli had said something that he kept going over in his head: professional storage facilities. It couldn't be just any storage facility; it had to be something that was secure. He would call Bob Morris, who was in Zurich working through the Lliessle Bank's books, and looking for bullion storage facilities. Using the phone was dangerous; it could be monitored. He hoped a burner phone might keep him off any surveillance.

• • •

The teams were spending the afternoon in the gym. For Ace, the run that morning had been more than enough exertion. He was in the library, a place where he had a legitimate reason to be.

The library was perfect for his research and even had a computer. He knew how to clear the files. First, he looked at the list of emails he couldn't read, then he looked up the gold storage facilities in Switzerland. Storage was available in the capital, Bern; in Zurich; and in the mountains.

Not really much help, he thought.

The burner phone was sitting beside him. Did Bazyli monitor the cell calls from the estate? He thought for a moment what that would take. Someone had to do the monitoring.

I've been everywhere on this estate. No one's doing any monitoring. It's very likely that Bazyli trusts his people. A fatal security flaw, thought Ace.

Instead of using the burner, he picked up the landline phone and called Bob.

"Ace, I'm still in Zurich. A lot to do here. What's going on? Oh, wait, Ace, I have another call I have to take. Will call you back in, say, a half hour."

Ace settled into one of the library's oversized leather chairs and gazed around the room. The books on the shelves had to be valuable. His problem was whether any of them were in English.

He got up and started to walk around the room, looking at titles. If the title was in English, then the book should be too. At first, all he saw were German books—and a few in Russian. At the back of the room, he found the English section.

On the top shelf was a row of books on World War II, the history and various battles. He saw what had to be a history of Austria and several books on German socialism. He pulled out one on politics. After all, Bazyli said he had to learn the history.

He flipped through several chapters, stopping at one that caught his eye, called "The Führer of Berlin."

After reunification, neo-Nazis in what had been Communist East Berlin began surfacing. The organized right-wing groups fought with the leftists and usually celebrated Hitler's birthday. Leaders marched in street protests beside far-right extremists.

Closing the book, he thought that the philosophy had to be primitive at best. Yet, he knew many people who were well educated believed in this philosophy. His problem was that he had been to several concentration camps—in particular Auschwitz. He knew decades later that the spirits of the dead remained in the ruins of the camp. The spirits spoke to him, and he believed they did to everyone who visited the camps.

Bob's call interrupted him. He spoke carefully, as they might be monitored. He was sure Bob would pick up on the word *decode*. Bob would know he meant *hacked*.

"Ace," said Bob, "I have just the program you need. Will send you the link."

"Can you send it to the phone number I'll give you?" asked Ace.

"Sure, let me know what it is."

Ace thanked him. "Bob, I hope we get to Zurich and catch up with you. Sending you the burner number now."

Back in the computer room, Ace downloaded the program Bob had sent to his burner phone to a flash drive and inserted it into the computer. He clicked on one of the emails to which he had been denied entry. A screen came up with a yes-or-no prompt. He clicked "Yes," and the email appeared.

Where did Bob get this program? wondered Ace.

Surely, the American intelligence agencies didn't hand them out to retirees. But he knew Bob had contacts. In Zurich, Bob would need such a program. His aunt was obsessed with the fact that her husband's files had not been fully reviewed.

One thing he and Amy had not looked at was the storage facility run by the Swiss government where account holders stored gold, jewels, and artwork. It was open only to the owners of storage areas inside. If Bob could break into it, then that would be a first. No one knew, or admitted they knew, whether the Count had stored something in it. Eighty years after the war, anyone who knew for sure was dead.

He turned back to reading the emails between Sig, Bazyli, and an unidentified third party. Nothing of interest was in the emails.

Bob's program had a directory for tracking the emails. Hitting that button, Ace found mention of Berlin. The third party was in Berlin, and at the bottom of the email, an address came up. He pulled out his phone and typed the address into his GPS.

"Wow," he said aloud.

The GPS showed the street in Berlin where the monastery was. Somehow, the old Abbot was a friend or an acquaintance of Sig and Bazyli.

After lunch, Ace returned to the computer room. He was curious about what Bazyli's team had been doing in Sylt. They were back; he had seen them running around the track. It didn't seem right to him that all they were doing was exercising.

He searched the emails—nothing. His burner phone rang, and he was glad he was alone in the room.

It was Amy. "We are back in Berlin, and Simon Bell told Sonora we need to go to Zurich and meet with Bob."

"Okay, I'll let Bazyli know. He says yes to anything Sonora wants, so I'll tell him she asked me to go. No problem getting there. The train across Austria goes right into Zurich."

Amy wasn't as sure about her trip. "I should be able to get a flight out tomorrow. See you soon."

"Do you know if Marton is in Berlin?"

"Haven't seen him, but Sonora and I plan to visit the Abbot."

• • •

Ace arrived at the station an hour before the train was due to leave. He was surprised to see Marton sitting in the eatery.

"Amy told me you would visit the eatery. It has the best coffee and strudel," said Marton. Ace waited to see what else Marton had to say.

Marton wanted information. He knew from German intelligence sources that Bazyli's boys had been in Sylt. Unfortunately, Ace didn't have any information.

"What I can tell you, Marton, is that some of the gold came here—just a few bars that Bazyli says were owed to his family from the Communist years. The rest from Husum went elsewhere. Zurich is the logical place for the gold. They have gold storage facilities. Both Bazyli and Amy seem to think that's where we'll find the gold. I'm meeting her in Zurich. To be honest, I'm not sure where to look or if we'll find it. You know how the Swiss are about gold. And gold that isn't even theirs."

Marton laughed. "Yes, I do. They will not readily give it up, even if they do not own it. I need to go back to Berlin. Not sure when we will meet again."

They shook hands, and Ace said, "See you soon."

• • •

Bazyli was still thinking about Ace going to Zurich. Ace managed to look innocent about finding the gold in the cave. Bazyli's gut told him Ace wasn't innocent. Now, what was in Zurich? He had to laugh. There was the Lliessle Bank, the gold storage facilities, and Bob Morris. So, what was Sonora's gang up to?

He picked up the phone and called Sig. "We have two guys who live and work in Zurich who have been watching the Lliessle villas. Whatever we do has to be very low-key. I don't want the Swiss police picking anyone up."

"Boss, they have been following Luca. He may run the Lliessle Bank, but so far, nothing he has done is unusual."

"Ace just called me and said his aunt needed him in Zurich. Something is up. I just smell it."

"All right," said Sig. "I can have Julian and Max focus on Amy and Ace rather than Luca. It is very likely that they both know some locals who can help. They would blend in. Both are slim and fit and just under six feet, and with their dark-brown hair and blue eyes, they look like typical Swiss businessmen. Not like spies or assassins or kidnappers."

Bazyli agreed.

"I will also call our staff in Zurich to reinforce just how important this surveillance is."

"Has Horst turned up yet?"

"No, sir. We expected him to arrive in Husum."

"Put out a missing persons request to Husum."

Sig said he would add Neustrelitz. "In the bar at the hotel, I heard Amy talking about how great the fish was, so they stopped there too."

Bazyli agreed. "I'd hate to lose him."

Bazyli hung up and poured more wine. Looking at the glass, he could see his profile, slightly clouded. He knew he would be drinking a lot more wine before they found out what the Prowers family was up to. Now, besides his son, he had another man, Horst, to avenge.

CHAPTER THIRTY-FOUR

Who Knew Where the Gold Was?

Amy wanted to fly back to Berlin, which involved changing planes in Hamburg. Thoren said driving would be just as fast.

And it was. They skipped tourist sights and arrived in Berlin at the Adlon Kempinski in just over four hours. Being back at the hotel seemed like she was home. A message was waiting for her; her aunt was coming for lunch at the hotel, and then they would be going to the monastery to meet with the Abbot.

While she waited for Sonora, she tried to watch the television news, but the German language for news was too complex for her. Fortunately, the images on the screen told her the news of the day.

She wondered what Bob Morris was doing. He had visited Sonora and now was back in Zurich. Had he learned anything about Switzerland's bullion storage facilities? She knew nothing about bullion storage sites in Switzerland. Were they regulated? How did they store the bullion? Could it be found? She would ask Bob when she saw him.

What was Ace doing? She hoped he wasn't getting into trouble. Nothing about joining Bazyli's group seemed safe to her.

She turned on the computer and searched *Raubgold*. The articles that came up made for interesting reading. One article was on how much gold was transferred to Switzerland during the war. The gold was taken from the national banks in the countries the Nazis occupied. They also took gold from private citizens in conquered countries and concentration camp victims. Part of it was used to finance Nazi Germany's military in World War II. Switzerland was the middleman. They took Nazi gold and paid other nations for their raw materials in Swiss francs. But the details of private transactions were difficult to identify. The reality today, according to the article, was that no one knew the extent of the transactions.

Gold came in many forms: bars, coins, and jewelry. It was accepted worldwide as a way to manage interbank transfers. Yet, gold was linked to the suffering of the victims of the Third Reich. Conspiracy theories abounded, including those about the accounts held by the Vatican Bank.

None of this was news to Amy. She'd heard it before. What she *did* learn was that in 1996, the US government began trying to identify countries and people who were responsible for gold transfers during World War II. Over a billion dollars was paid by Swiss banks to the families of those who had died in the concentration camps. How did they identify the victims fifty years after the war? She bet Bob would know.

Reading on, she found that Zurich had both gold and silver bullion vaults. She learned that Swiss gold vaults required four hundred troy ounces of gold in each bar. The Zurich silver vault required a thousand troy ounces in a bar. The minimum assayed purity for both was ninety-nine-point-nine percent and was used by dealers in the Swiss bullion market.

Enough for now, she thought, but an article on the German election caught her eye.

In Brandenburg, the state surrounding Berlin, the AfD made gains in the last German election. It doubled the vote in that state and tripled its support in the state of Saxony to the south. The AfD gained support from young voters, but the main parties, like the Christian Democratic Union Party, said that they would not form a coalition with right-wing groups. She had to wonder how long that would last if right-wingers were gaining power.

Lunch was chicken schnitzel and a bottle of one of Germany's finest Rieslings at the Adlon Kempinski. Amy poured the remainder of the wine into her glass and said to Sonora, "After the four-hour drive from Husum, this meal has me ready to meet the Abbot. Do you think he's going to be honest with us?"

"I hope so." Sonora sounded optimistic.

"Why should he tell us the truth? He has a lot to lose."

Sonora laughed. "You don't think an Abbot would be honest?"

"Never."

They both laughed.

"Amy, if he has the gold, why would he keep it? How can the Abbot use it? What's he going to spend it on? The Abbot's family is wealthy, and with Misha dead, he's the last living descendant of his family. Everyone else died in the war. I know the Abbot doesn't feel any loyalty to the Vatican. He told me once when the Berlin Wall was up that he felt betrayed, not by the pope but by the group of religion-mongers who surround him.

"Would he hold on to both family money and the gold? What would he do with it? I know he's not supposed to own any-thing, but I suspect he hasn't given it all back to the Benedictine Order or to the church. He's extremely independent. Well, that's my take on him, knowing him all these years."

"At least he's willing to see us," said Amy.

Sonora agreed. "I called. He's expecting us. But something else concerns me." She wasn't sure how to bring up this topic but knew she had to. Her niece wasn't the only gold treasure hunter in Europe. Many of them had been searching for decades.

"Amy, how long are you going to keep looking for the gold? I love having you in Berlin because you can run the Prowers busi-ness from here. You must realize that the gold may be gone— even Vince couldn't find it. Tell me, how are you going to know when to stop the search?"

"I'll know. I'll feel it inside." She laughed. "Maybe Vince will tell me."

"That I understand," said Sonora.

"The bank trust can manage the oil and gas leases," said Amy, "and I can manage our overall portfolio from here. You know I love Berlin and Switzerland. I'd say by late winter, if we don't find the gold, I'll be back at the condo in Vail. Maybe I can convince you to come visit. The mountains will be covered in snow, and we'll be able to ski or just ride the gondolas to the restaurants on the mountaintops."

Sonora said she was ready to visit Colorado. What she didn't say was how relieved she was that Amy realized that she might not find the gold.

Amy asked, "Have you talked to Bob Morris? Has he found anything in Zurich on gold being stored in Swiss bullion vaults?"

"Nothing yet, Amy. You and Ace have to go back to Switzerland. I hope Ace has already left. Maybe Bob will have found something by then. I know he was frustrated. I told him that when you're dealing with the Swiss, nothing is transparent."

"He likes action, conclusions," said Amy. "I'm looking forward to going back to Switzerland. Somewhere, stored in that country, I believe is the gold that has been taken from the mudflats in Husum."

Sonora agreed. Yet, she knew Switzerland wasn't a country that readily gave up its secrets.

CHAPTER THIRTY-FIVE

Meeting the Abbot

The Prowers family was due any minute, but the Abbot wanted to call Luca. He'd been working for the Lliessle family in Zurich when the monastery monks, led by Frederic, took the gold from the monastery to Switzerland. Then, he realized there was no need to call. Luca, if he knew, would never tell him.

The question was why Frederic had brought the gold to the monastery in the first place. When the gold arrived at the monastery from Husum, he was on a retreat in Greece. The old Abbot stored it for a day or so for Frederic. Then, with the help of the monks, they moved the gold to Switzerland. Only a month after the gold had been moved, the old Abbot died.

As he looked back, he didn't see a problem in sharing this with the Prowers women. The more honest he appeared, the more they would believe him when he wasn't honest. He'd even show them the tunnels where the gold had been temporarily stored. Only his brother Misha, who coordinated the shipment for the Abbot, knew how much had been shipped to Bazyli Czartoryski. Sonora and Amy didn't need that information.

The coffee was brewing, a Malawian specialty that one of the brothers had brought back from Africa. The women would appreciate it. Maybe they would be distracted. Maybe not. Neither one of them was naïve. He had to handle them with care.

What about the Vatican's role in the stolen gold? Should I bring it up? I always believed Count Lliessle was involved with the gold transfers through the Vatican. Too many monks and priests kept visiting the Count's villa in Zurich during World War II.

The Count was rich. He didn't need the gold and could afford to leave it stored. That made him almost invincible. Nazis, former Nazis—especially the SS, Hitler's personal security service—needed money at the end of the war. To escape Europe, money was needed for bribing officials, and to establish a new life and identity.

Who would know if the Count had kept some of the gold? The Lliessle Bank handled transfers for the Vatican. It would have been easy to transfer some funds into a personal account. If the Count did, then who knew today where it was?

Did he tell his wife? How much did Sonora know about her husband's banking business? True, she was much younger, *my age*, he thought. Still the Count should have told his wife. He wasn't sure, but he had to take the chance that the old Swiss Count hadn't kept his wife in the dark.

When Amy and Sonora arrived, the monastery smelled like freshly brewed coffee.

"The sitting room is lovely. You've renovated it since I was here," said Sonora.

"Yes, one of the monks did it." He poured the coffee and asked the obvious. "The gold was not in Husum?"

"No."

Amy was tired of all the chitchat and decided to tell him the truth, though she suspected he already knew. "It had been stored in the mudflats until about five years ago, when it was taken away in a couple of trips by Frederic and some monks. The locals said they thought the gold was going to Berlin. Your brother Misha implied it was here. I just didn't pick up on what he was saying to me before he was killed."

Now, it was Sonora's turn. "Your monastery is on the border of what was once East Germany. The area is known for its tunnels, which the East Germans used to escape. The tunnels would be a natural storage area for gold."

The Abbot nodded yes, and addressed her informally, as she had told him to. "Sonora, over the decades, and before I even joined the order, you and your husband have been loyal supporters of our monastery. I can show you the tunnels where the gold Frederic brought from Husum was stored. It is just below our brewery operation."

"Was?" asked Sonora.

"Yes, was." The Abbot said that the gold had stayed in the monastery for only a few weeks. Then, Frederic and the monks hauled it away.

"I was in Greece when the monks returned. I asked where they had gone and was told Switzerland. The old Abbot seemed to think it went to the Lliessle Bank in Zurich."

"A good story," said Sonora. "Zurich maybe, but I doubt it made it to the bank. We'll take you at your word, Abbot, and skip the tunnels."

The Abbot realized that this was his moment, and he had to take it. "Sonora, what about the Count's dealings with the Vatican?"

Sonora didn't evade his question. She was surprisingly forthcoming. "So far, there have been a lot of leads to follow up. I know my husband dealt with the Vatican and that Lliessle Bank handled Vatican transfers."

The Abbot asked if she knew about accounts the Lliessle Bank held for the Vatican Bank. For a moment, Sonora looked disgusted. "Of course. The Count told me that the Vatican Bank needed to use the banks in Switzerland because the Vatican was on the list of noncooperative countries, which meant it didn't meet international banking standards. It wasn't until this century, sometime in 2010, that the Vatican Bank was compliant with international banking standards. For many years, their actions were totally secretive and in the interests of Rome and their account holders."

The Abbot agreed. "Today, the Vatican has accounts in Swiss banks. Some is the gold they had before World War II, which is now stored in the bullion vaults. They needed Switzerland because the Vatican Bank was not created until 1940."

He paused before saying that no one knew where the gold went, other than to Argentina. Perón, who had supported the Nazis, ran the country from the end of World War II into the early 1950s.

Then, the Abbot laughed. "That is the nature of banking. Bankers don't care where the money comes from or where it goes. Enough said."

Amy listened to the Abbot and her aunt casually discuss the transfers that had happened so many decades ago. Was everyone so blasé about past events that still affected lives today?

She knew that Vince was committed to finding the gold because he was committed to finding the truth. After he stumbled on the bag in the forest in England, he believed it was his destiny to search for the gold. He didn't do it for the money. The gold to him represented the lives of those who died.

He told her he had a plan for the gold but wouldn't say what it was; he said he'd tell her once it was found. She always suspected he'd give it back to the survivors and spend years tracking them down. But she didn't know for sure. If it was up to her, then she'd establish a foundation and make donations to those in need who were the descendants of those killed.

She watched the Abbot pour more coffee. Both he and her aunt were part of the past. Without asking, she knew that they both believed in their destinies.

What, she wondered, *is my destiny?*

The Abbot paused, sipped coffee, and asked her aunt another question. It was one Amy had wondered about for some time.

"Surely, the Count would have told you where the gold was?"

Sonora's face turned up, and she looked like she was going to say, "You're kidding."

Very unlike her, thought Amy.

Instead, Sonora said, "If he had, we wouldn't be spending all this time looking for it."

"Perhaps a clue?" asked the Abbot.

She shook her head. "Believe me, I've thought about where it could be. Did he indicate where it might be? Truth is, we never talked about it. He left for Zurich with Frederic and Marton's father, came back, and died two weeks later."

"I only ask," said the Abbot, "because to me, it seems odd that he would not tell you where the gold was. So much gold, and what it is worth in today's prices . . . a fortune, for sure."

Sonora didn't feel like discussing her relationship with her husband with the Abbot yet realized she had to convince him she didn't know the location. "Abbot, if I knew where it was, would I be putting my niece and myself through this circus?"

Amy realized that the trip hadn't been a waste of time. The Abbot would never have told them the truth over the phone. The monastery had a landline, and after all those years living in East Germany, he believed it was monitored. Maybe it was.

One thing she had learned was that she was certain that Sonora didn't know where the gold was. Like the Abbot, she found it strange that as close as Sonora and the Count were, he hadn't told her. Or at least left her a clue.

Vince never found the gold. And she was beginning to doubt whether she'd find it. If Sonora didn't know, then who did?

She shook her head as if to forget her memories. It was time to fly to Zurich and join Ace and Bob in the search for the storage vault.

. . .

How many years had passed since Simon Bell had spoken to Sonora? It had been at least five years since the Count had died. How long had they known each other?

Sonora said, "At my age, all the years seem to run together."

But Simon remembered. "Thirty years, Mrs. Lliessle."

They looked at each other, both thinking how fast the years had gone. With his white-blond hair and fair complexion, Simon had aged well.

Seated in the living room of the hotel apartment, Sonora opened a bottle of red wine, an exquisite Italian, and poured it into two glasses. She knew that Simon, though raised in a beer-drinking world, preferred red wine. She wanted information from Simon, and drinking wine was a starter.

Simon was way ahead of her. "Sonora, most of the gold went to Switzerland when Frederic took it out of the mudflats, where he had stored it decades before." He went on to say that Frederic, with his financial contacts, had gotten access to the gold that had been stored in the Reichsbank in Berlin. The Nazi gold was kept in the bank until near the end of World War II, when it was moved. He thought that it was probably moved by the monks at the end of the war because Berlin was in chaos.

"I do not know who moved it but believe after the war, it was stored in the monastery. The monk Misha, who Amy met in Vilnius, and the Abbot knew it was there and did nothing. The monastery was in East Germany, and it was difficult to move anything out, even for monks. Questions would have been raised, especially with the Russians, so it was left in the monastery for several decades until the wall separating East and West Germany came down in 1989. When it was safe to move, Frederic took it to Husum and buried it in the mudflats. How Frederic knew it was in the monastery, no one seems to know."

He looked at Sonora. "The irony is that it was Frederic who brought it back from Husum, stored the trucks overnight at the monastery, and left the next morning for Switzerland. At least, that is what everyone thinks, including me."

Sonora said she agreed with his analysis. "I was in and out of the country and was not in Berlin when Frederic came through Berlin with the gold. Luca, who runs our bank in Zurich, would know." She paused. "Unless it was done off the books. Then, Luca wouldn't know."

She wasn't sure Luca would tell them the truth. It all happened so many years ago. Who knew what the truth was?

After Simon left, Sonora called Marton, who arrived at the hotel within the hour. For once, she was pleased that they had the apartment at the hotel. Meetings were easy to set up with the hotel being centrally located in Berlin.

"Marton, why don't you go to Zurich?"

He wasn't sure. "Is there something you would like me to do there?"

"Yes, the villas we own in Zurich are important. They are large, but they cannot hold all the gold from Husum. That means the gold is in a Swiss gold storage facility, or it should be. The Count was very security conscious and wouldn't have stored the gold unless he was sure it was safe."

She went on to say that the Count had said he and Marton's father had gone to Zurich to assist Frederic. "My gut tells me that all three knew where it was stored. Frederic could never have stored the gold alone. My husband and your father helped him. The irony is that no one seems to have seen them in Zurich. They weren't invisible, so what happened to those trucks?"

She paused. They both were thinking the same thing: how did they just disappear in Zurich?

"Marton, the gold cannot be far from Zurich. The Count would never have been driving along those winding mountain roads. He always took the train. You can do me a favor: go to Zurich and find out what is going on, not just with my niece and nephew but also what Bazyli's men are doing. They all have to be there watching our villas. I will pay for the plane ticket. No train."

He smiled. "I do spend a lot of time on trains."

As he spoke, Marton realized that Simon would be pleased he was working for Sonora. "I'll let you know if I come up with any information on the gold."

CHAPTER THIRTY-SIX

In Zurich

The Lliessle villas in Zurich were two residences side by side with separate entrances. The Count designed them and loved the deception. No one knew the Lliessle family owned both. One villa was used for visitors and was almost a duplicate of the first. There was only one difference; it didn't have a staff, butler, or cook.

Ace checked the refrigerator. It was stacked with wine, vegetables, and what looked like precooked meals. "Bob, you've been on your own here?"

"Yes, since I got back from Berlin." He held up his phone and tapped a message, holding it up for Ace to read: "I think the villa is bugged." Ace nodded that he understood.

"The villa has a lot of space, separate bedroom apartments for guests. We could ask Luca for a cook."

Bob said he had been eating his main meals at the other villa. "Luca's cook is excellent."

Ace and Amy looked at each other.

"Works for us," said Amy. "We ate there when we were here before."

"Great. The apartments are up the stairs. Settle in and meet me on the patio. The view is spectacular. We can't waste a nice sunset."

When Amy and Ace joined him, Bob was sipping an Italian red wine and looking over the cheese and pizza slices that the cook had brought over from the other villa. He raised his glass.

"This is great wine. Though we're in the German part of Switzerland, I felt compelled to sample wine from the Italian sector."

Amy and Ace filled their wine glasses and lifted them in a toast, and then it was time to get down to business—the business of finding where the gold was stored. Amy asked how much gold was involved. So far, no one seemed to know.

Bob explained, sounding quite cheerful considering he didn't know where the gold was stored. Luca had told him Frederic and the monks brought at least eighty bags from Germany. A few bars are stored in the main villa. "Where the rest is, Luca says he has no clue. When he gets back from his errands, he'll show us what's in the house. Where the rest of the gold is the problem."

He paused. "Most of the German gold reserves were kept at the Reichsbank in Berlin. The last two years of the war, when the Allies began bombing Berlin, much of the gold bullion and

Reichsmarks were dispersed to branch banks in central and southern Germany.

"O.K., what has been found. We can thank the Germans for keeping such detailed records. You've heard about the Merkers salt mine about two hundred miles south of Berlin?"

"Yes."

"I'll skip over the several hundred containers of artwork that was found. The gold consisted of eight thousand three hundred gold bars and fifty-five boxes of gold bullion. There were bags of gold coins—over three thousand, I believe—and eight bags of gold rings. Sixty-three bags of silver were also found—and one bag of platinum bars. It was quite a haul. And found thanks to a couple of female French expats who, when American army men gave them a ride, causally mentioned the gold stored in the salt mine."

Bob poured more wine for everyone. Continuing his story, he said that other gold assets were sent to Berlin. The Schutzstaffel, or SS, Office for Economy and Administration ran the concentration camps. From 1942 to January 1945, some seventy-six deliveries of gold were made to the Reichsbank, from property seized from the concentration camp victims.

The gold was deposited in the Reichsbank in the name of Melmer, the captain who made most of the deliveries to Berlin from the east. From there, it was transferred to the Prussian Mint or Degussa, the German industrial firm that refined precious metals. When the transactions were completed, the deposits were credited to the account of a Max Heiliger, the code name for Heinrich Himmler and his SS. By 1945, most of the deposits had been transferred to other banks, but a significant amount of gold was still in Berlin. With Berlin being bombed, it was shipped to Merkers.

"Think of what was found in Merkers that hadn't been melted down. Cigarette cases, diamonds, gold and silver coins and bars, along with dental work filled over one hundred eighty-nine suitcases and trunks."

Ace interrupted, "So, the SS realized the war was over."

"Yes. Some thought they would make a stand in the Alps. But the Allied army moved rapidly, and they couldn't get organized."

Bob looked at Amy. "You asked how much gold. Well, in 1945, it was thought to be about a half billion dollars. Today, it's worth much more. In 1934, gold was thirty-five dollars an ounce. Today, it's about two thousand dollars an ounce. Now, a ton of gold has about thirty-two thousand ounces in it. No one can be sure about the number of tons, but the value is in the billions. How much is missing? No one knows."

Ace was doing some math. "Given the number of trucks it took for Frederic and the monks to haul the gold out of Husum, it has to be in the billions. Worst case, it could be only a few hundred million. Just guessing of course."

The three laughed.

"How it works is a guess," said Amy. "What's true is that today, the value would be astronomical. Now, where's the gold Frederic brought to Switzerland? Bob, you said you knew."

Bob threw up his hands. "More or less. I know it's in one of the Swiss bullion storage facilities or in a private storage facility. Sounds good, huh? Problem is, where? The security to get into these sites is unbelievable, and they're all over Switzerland. I have one we can visit tomorrow. Luca gave us a referral."

He paused for a moment, then added, "I just saw Luca's car pull in. Now, we need to see the gold that's in the other villa."

Ace was the product of his background. "To me, this looks like a smoke screen, hiding some in the Lliessle house. Wherever the gold is, there must be roads or an airfield into the site. Or it could be here in a Zurich bullion storage site, right under our noses. Surely, Luca knows."

Bob shook his head. "He claims he doesn't. All he knows is there's a tunnel under the house in which the gold is stored. Luca says that gold belongs to the Lliessle Bank and was stored here before World War II. It is not *Raubgold*, what the Nazis stole."

Amy sipped her drink, then spoke. "Someone—the Count or Marton's father—who worked here knows. I guess I should say *did* know, as they're dead, and Frederic may be too."

Remembering the Count's personality, she knew he loved secrets. He was a cautious man, not reckless. He must have left a clue somewhere. Perhaps the clue was so oblique that no one, not even her aunt, could recognize it as a clue.

The phone rang.

"It's Luca," said Bob. "Let's see what gold is stored in the house."

They left the visitors villa and walked about forty feet to Luca's villa next door. The night was clear and cold. Bob couldn't help but notice a car parked farther down the road.

Though there were other large homes along the road, cars were never parked outside the gates. The Swiss were very exacting, some would say fussy. Cars were usually parked inside the villa's gates because the police would ticket them on the street. He had been here long enough to know a parked car was unusual.

The license plate was shaded in the darkness. It was a small but expensive sedan. No point in worrying the Prowers family. When he got back to the mansion, he would reset the security cameras to look at the street, not the villas' driveway.

Luca wasted no time taking them to where the gold was stored. He explained that there had been an old staircase, but the Count had replaced it with a small elevator.

"The elevator will not hold all of us."

Ace went down first with Luca, who sent the elevator back up for Bob and Amy. They were in a wine cellar, with one wall filled with wine bottles to the ceiling.

"Useful," said Ace. "Wine and gold."

Luca laughed. "The wine was here long before the gold."

The screeching of the elevator's ropes told them that it was back with Amy and Bob.

Luca said to follow him. "The gold is in a separate room that is locked."

After walking past more cases filled with wine, they reached a room with steel bars and huge padlocks on the door. "Security may look weak," said Luca, "but realize that a thief has to get into the house first, then find the elevator and get down here." He turned the keys in the lock, removed the bars, and opened the door.

Inside was a small table with a lamp. In the center of the room was a lump covered with heavy canvas. Removing the canvas revealed the gold.

Fifteen gold bars were stacked in groups of five. Luca said they had the exact dimensions of the Reichsbank gold bars. Each was a quarter inch thick, one and three-quarter inches wide, and four inches long. Luca handed one to Amy.

"It is heavy for its size—weighs just over two pounds."

"Yes, and each is engraved with the words 'Deutsche Reichsbank' on the top." She gently put the bar back on the stack.

Luca said each bar was worth about sixty-seven thousand dollars. "We round the price of gold, which makes the math easier, to two thousand dollars an ounce. These bars are estimated to be worth just over a million dollars."

He went on to say that the value of gold went up and down over the years. "The gold in the Merkers mine was worth two hundred forty-one million dollars based on thirty-five dollars an ounce. Based on today's value of two thousand dollars an ounce, the Merkers gold would be worth almost thirty-four billion. The Allies believed the gold in the Merkers mine was about ninety percent of all the gold in circulation after the war. Today, it appears they were mistaken."

Luca laughed, something he didn't do often. "The Count and Frederic knew what they were doing. How much gold they had is anyone's guess. What I know is the Count was a banker and on the board of other Swiss banks. The gold held in banks in individual accounts has never been found. You think these bankers did not know who ended up in concentration camps and died without death certificates? Of course, they knew."

Luca paused, then went on, "Next, there is the question of the gold from concentration camps. No one has any idea how much gold that might be. Until all of it is found, the amount will continue to be a guess."

Ace picked up one of the bars. "They're heavy but pocket-size." He looked at the "Reichsbank" engraved on each. The bars didn't leave much to the imagination.

Bob was more sanguine. "We'll never find the stored gold without some clue or a lot of luck. The good news is no one else will either."

"What's next?" asked Amy.

Bob shrugged. "Ace, maybe you should go back to Bazyli's Vienna training site. It's obvious he doesn't know where the gold is hidden. He's looking for answers. You could at least find out where they're searching."

"If Frederic was alive, we'd know where to find it. Does any-one really know what happened to him?" asked Ace.

Bob watched Luca, who was silent.

Amy shook her head. "Thoren says only his mother believes he's still alive. But that's what a mother would think. Did Sonora ever see the trucks with the gold?"

Bob said she had told him no.

"The trucks came here," said Luca. "I remember Frederic picking up the Count and Marton's father. They left, and no one seems to know where they went."

Amy had heard enough. "It's been a long day. Let's eat dinner and hit the bullion bunker trail tomorrow. Thank you, Luca, for the reference to the vault."

"I suggest a drink before you go back to the other villa," said Luca. "We can discuss how to look for other storage vaults. The bars in this villa are only a fraction of what Frederic brought from Husum. And like I said, who can say what the Count already had stored."

No one objected to a drink before dinner.

Amy was glad Luca had such good wine, another Italian red. As she sipped it, she wondered if he was anti-French. Now, she, Ace, and Bob would get his take on Swiss gold vaults. And he didn't disappoint them.

"The storage areas were built as military bunkers. In World War Two, over twenty thousand bunkers were built to fortify our little nation against the Nazis. Today supposedly, there are still over one thousand usable bunkers. In the 1991, when the Cold War was supposed to be over, the Swiss government opened them up to the public. Some are owned by banks, and some are used as tourist attractions.

"Did you know that an individual from any nation can own one? The bullion vaults don't have numbered accounts, but need a real person or an organization to back them up. Still some undesirables get in. The ones owned by banks and by investment brokers charge in the millions for individuals to store their gold. Who stored it, and what is in it, only the owner knows. At least one bunker is near an old airfield, and the clients fly in."

As he took a sip of wine, Bob interrupted. "Luca, what about the bullion storage vaults here and in Bern?"

Luca said the storage vault in Zurich was protected by the Swiss government. It existed during World War II but was always under the control of the Swiss government. It wasn't far from the villas, even though it was in an industrial area. His next point was the most important.

"The Count used to go to that storage vault at least once a week. He also went up to the mountains every month."

Ace asked if Luca had any idea what identification or codes the Count used to get into the vaults.

"No way to know, and security is tight at those vaults. I worked for the Count for decades and have no idea where he stored the gold."

Amy asked how the Count knew Frederic.

"Financial firms, brokage deals," said Luca. "Frederic was a broker for the Count, and that is how they met. It is not usually mentioned, but the Count had an extensive stock portfolio, international and in America."

"You think Frederic knew the codes where the gold was stored?" asked Amy.

Luca was positive he did. "And do not forget it was Frederic who brought the gold out of Husum to Zurich."

After that comment, Bob suggested that they go back to the villa for dinner. "I know, Luca, your cook will send over a tasty meal. Everything I have eaten here has been great."

"Thank you," said Luca.

Amy told him they appreciated his help.

Bob said, "Until next time."

They all knew there would be a next time.

CHAPTER THIRTY-SEVEN

Gold Storage Facilities

Back at the villa, drinking brandy as a nightcap, Bob Morris wasn't excited about finding gold storage facilities. He'd read enough to realize how tough—or, to put it bluntly, futile—it would be.

"The Swiss built storage bunkers in the mountains before and during World War II. Today, Zurich and Bern have government-protected, secure warehouses. Luca said they are fortresses. Takes special codes to get in. Nothing happens fast with these people. The Swiss are not forthcoming, if I can use that word."

"Does this mean we're at a dead end? I don't want to sound negative, but if the search is over, it's over, right?"

Amy sounded concerned, but she also knew a dead end was dead. Vince's dream of finding the gold seemed to be over. Vince thought the gold was still out there, and so did she. But without clues, the search was over.

Bob sipped his German brandy. He thought their brandies had more flavor, more body. "No, it isn't the end. We need to look at history to figure out what happened to the gold. For instance, in 2013, the Swiss distributed payments to the survivors of the Holocaust, fifteen years after the agreement to make payments was signed in 1998. The Swiss made the payments because the major Swiss banks wanted access to the American markets to expand their business. To get access, they signed an agreement to pay Holocaust survivors and their families over a billion dollars. No one knows how much money is still in the banks from survivors of World War II, including German military and civilian accounts."

"That's where they failed, finding the survivors," said Amy. "I remember how they wanted death certificates from people who died in the concentration camps, when none were ever given."

Ace was tired of hearing about the history of the gold. "What about today and the bullion storage vaults? I know the Swiss reputation for secrecy, privacy, security, whatever you want to call it. How do we break through that wall?"

Ace was on the computer. "Our problem is, where are the Count's passwords? Amy, would he have given them to Sonora? I don't think he would have trusted anyone else."

Amy said her aunt didn't seem to have a clue where the gold might be. "She told me and the Abbot that we wouldn't be playing games with this search if she knew."

Bob said it might depend on two factors: whether Frederic was alive and whether they could find him. "While you were at Husum, Luca and I had dinner every night. One night, after several bottles of wine, he told me that he had seen Frederic on one of Zurich's main streets. He said if it wasn't Frederic, it had to be his twin. Whoever it was disappeared down a side street. Luca wasn't able to catch him."

Ace laughed. "Our stoic Swiss was drunk?"

"I guess so; otherwise, I don't think he'd have mentioned it. Though, come to think of it, maybe Frederic is one of those people who continues to be seen whether he's there or not, or dead or alive."

While they were talking, Ace had been looking out the bay windows at the front of the house. He was watching an old man with a walking stick walk up and down the street. He finally disappeared around the corner.

"I've been watching this guy who looks old go up and down the street. But I really don't think he is old. Is he a local? Down the street is a neighborhood café. I guess that's where he went. The car we noticed earlier is still parked up the street."

Bob said using a car sounded like something Bazyli would do for surveillance. He got up and looked out the window with Ace. For now, there was nothing they could do.

"I'm not sure Bazyli thinks Frederic's dead," said Ace. "He seemed to think I could find him."

Bob shook his head. "It's very likely that he's dead, killed on a safari or in some other place in Africa. It's a big continent. If he was alive, he would be with the gold."

"This is a dead end. I'm ready to go back to Berlin," said Amy. "I'd like to think that even Vince would have stopped searching now. I mean, there has to be a limit to what we can do. Vince might keep looking, but I'm about done. I mean, where else can we look?"

Bob laughed and said that somewhere, fifty years from now, someone would stumble across the gold. "But let's go up the mountain and take a look at a couple of the storage bunkers—or vaults, as they call them today. The Swiss seem to think vaults are more valuable, and they charge more for their use. We can drive by the bullion vault in Zurich. At least we can say we did something."

They all agreed.

"Then, back to Berlin," said Amy. "And hopefully, forget about the gold."

"Never," Ace and Bob said in unison.

"I'm going to call Sonora, even though I don't know what she can add to our search," said Amy.

"Call tomorrow," said Bob. "It's late, and you've both had a long day. But one last thing, what are you going to do if we find the gold?"

Amy had the answer and it was so simple. The Prowers family would set up a trust fund to verify descendants of the victims and to make payments to them.

To herself, she was bothered that some of the gold had been personal jewelry, melted down from the concentration camp victims. That was the secret gold held; no one could ever tell where it came from. There was no way to really make payments fair.

For now, she was tired, and there were no answers. She thought, *I'm giving up this search, even if Vince wouldn't. Somethings have to end."*

Maybe they would learn something at the storage facilities. Maybe.

Amy placed the call to Sonora using her cell phone. Ace suggested she use it because no one might be tracking it. She explained to her aunt that they were at a dead end.

"Amy, the gold must be close to Zurich. I can't see the Count traipsing over the mountain roads. Not his style."

"So, we should check bunkers around Zurich?"

"Yes. And remember, he always took the train."

"Okay," said Amy.

Sonora pointed out that Zurich, the financial center, and Bern, the capital, were only about seventy-five miles apart. Both cities were convenient for moving gold and silver in the country or out of it.

Sonora said, "These two cities would be the logical place to hide the gold."

Amy thanked her and turned to the guys to repeat what she had said.

"Back to the map of bunkers, I mean storage vaults, to plot our trip tomorrow," said Bob.

CHAPTER THIRTY-EIGHT

Into the Swiss Alps

While Bob, Amy, Ace, and Luca were enjoying dinner, Marton was in his room in a cheap hotel on the edge of Zurich, preparing to go out for the second time that evening. He looked at the crack in the mirror. Fortunately, the mirror was still big enough for him to see that the hairpiece and fake beard were in place.

Bazyli's men had to be watching the Lliessle villas. He was also sure that somewhere within the walls of the villas, the Count must have left a clue as to where the gold was stored. *Hidden* was a word he thought more likely, though it implied that owning the gold might be illegal.

After the war, there were estimates of how much gold had been spent by the Nazis to run the war and how much was left.

He knew the estimates were wrong. His father told him that they were wrong and that he and the Count hid the gold. His father just didn't say where.

Was Frederic dead? He must be. He hadn't been seen since he left for South Africa five years ago. Before he left, when the Count was still alive, Frederic had moved the gold from Husum to Switzerland. Not for a moment did Marton think it had been stored in Germany. With over a thousand active bunkers left over from the war, Marton knew the gold had to be stored in Switzerland.

The Count and his father were cautious men. They would have left a clue somewhere or with someone. But with whom? And where? He didn't know. The good news was neither did anyone else. If Bazyli knew, then he would have found the gold by now.

This was his second trip to survey the two Lliessle villas. Picking up his walking cane, he practiced his limp. He was ready to walk down the street again.

An expensive sedan was now parked at the end of the street under a row of trees. Bazyli likely had paid off the local police to allow the sedan to park there, as the Swiss didn't allow parking on the street in such an exclusive residential area. They said it was for security reasons.

To the left was a trail that led into a wildlife area. Two of Bazyli's men were sitting inside, alternating four-hour shifts. They had been surveying the Lliessle villas for over a week and hadn't noticed anything outside the usual comings and goings and deliveries. Today, their efforts paid off.

On the north side of the road, around a curve, was a local café, bar, and outdoor patio. A man had been walking around the block, disappearing once or twice into the café. When they first saw him, they thought he was a local walking to the café. On his third walk around the block, the men decided it was odd. They were both sure he was interested in the Lliessle villas. Sig had told them to pick up anyone who seemed to be watching the villas.

The two men looked at each other.

"Should we flip?"

"No, I will go. He has a limp. Cannot be too tough to pick up. We have practiced these pickups at Bazyli's training."

Marton saw the two men coming toward him but knew he was as fast today as he had been twenty years ago. He could handle two men; he was sure. But he hadn't counted on how aggressive and fit they might be. When the man reached out to grab him, he broke away and ran to the end of the street, down the walking trail, and into the wildlife area. The two men were right behind him.

As the trail curved, they caught up with him. Marton pulled out a knife and immediately took out one man. He was hurt but not dead. Unfortunately, the second man had time to grab Marton from behind, and within seconds, his neck was broken.

The men knew they had to conceal the body. No way did they want the Swiss police or someone walking their dog to find it. They dragged it under the trees, just off the path, and covered it with branches.

"We will come back tonight when it is dark and pick it up."

They could not allow the Swiss authorities to find the body. The authorities would flood the area with police and investigators and their surveillance would also cease.

CHAPTER THIRTY-NINE

Into the Swiss Alps

The next morning, Bob, Amy, and the driver, Julian, were heading to the mountain storage site.

Ace had decided to stay at the villa. He had found a row of accounting books on a bottom shelf in the study. No one had looked at these records, and maybe they were important.

"I'm comfortable in the house, and the food is good," Ace said.

"Okay. See you when we get back." Amy was eager to get started, having no idea what they might find but not feeling very optimistic.

"First, we drive by the biggest bullion storage vault in Zurich," said Bob. "Then, we head up the mountains to a former bunker, now a bullion vault."

Amy was looking at a map as Bob outlined the trip to one of the main vaults on the south side of Zurich. Slowly, the car passed the armed guards and barbwire fence around the large cement building said to be the bullion storage vault in Zurich.

"No way anyone can get into the vaults without identification," said Amy. Bob agreed.

Amy was still wondering about their Swiss driver, Julian. Just because someone worked at the Lliessle Bank didn't mean they were trustworthy. She knew they needed someone who spoke German and French—but still.

I see Switzerland as a country of secrets, she thought.

She asked Julian, "Are you a native of Zurich?"

"Yes," he said, "I have lived here all my life."

He didn't mention that he had gone to school in Vienna, which was where he met Sig. They had been in the same class and had played football together. Sig had called that morning to give him a heads-up that Luca would be asking him to play chauffeur. Sig said it was important to keep track of where they went and what was said. He knew he would have to report, so he listened intently to their conversations.

The day was sunny but cold. The mountains were covered in snow, but the snow had melted on the road. They passed through several picture-perfect villages. Amy felt like she was on a tour; Bob was focused on the road.

"This vault we're heading to is one of the biggest and is less than an hour from Zurich. They have an airfield and a hotel. Luca has paved the way, as not just anyone can get into these places." He looked at Amy. "Fortunately, the Prowers and Lliessle fortunes are enough wealth to let us gain entry."

They turned off the highway, following a twisting, narrow road. Large iron gates stopped their progress.

The gates slowly opened, and a mountain appeared in front of them. A few hundred yards up the road, they were in front of a modern Alpine hotel. Beside it was the office for the vault, complete with a sign that said "Office." The manager, Wilhelm, was expecting them.

Wilhelm looked like a Swiss gentleman of about forty. Trim and slim, dressed in gray pants and a matching tunic jacket, he was barely taller than Amy. She noticed that he walked with what she thought was a military bearing.

Wilhelm welcomed them; Luca had called and told him they were prospective customers. He said they were not allowed in any of the secure areas, but a video would show them what these areas looked like.

"Before we watch the video, I would like to take you to the door of the vault. Give you an idea of what our security is like. It is our priority," he said.

They followed him out a side door and onto a cement path leading into the side of a large mountain, the top of which couldn't be seen. After passing through a huge steel gate that was open, he stopped at an iron door buried in the rock of the mountain, the kind one would see in a bank vault. It was surrounded by lights, with a phone and keypad mounted to one side. On either side of the door stood two men in black fatigues, armed with pistols and automatic weapons, which were slung over their shoulders.

"Switzerland is famous for its banks. Unknown to many people is that we have storage vaults buried under the mountains. These men do eight-hour shifts around the clock, and those doors are blast-proof and weigh over three tons. This bunker has been here for over fifty years."

"Why build here?" asked Bob.

"During World War II, thousands of bunkers were built to counter an attack by the German Army. Though we were neutral, the Nazis were invading every country around us. Our leaders built these bunkers and stocked them with weapons and supplies for soldiers in case of a German attack.

"The mountains hid tanks, aircraft, and artillery guns, some pointed at our own roads to destroy them in case of invasion. A small number of Swiss could fight off anything the Nazis threw at us. We would never have surrendered to the Nazis."

Wilhelm paused for a moment. "Then, it all changed because the world changed. It was in 1991s, when the Cold War was said to be over. The government sold these bunkers, really fortresses, to companies to use any way they wanted. Some are just tourist attractions. One high-tech bank sells space for digital records.

"It is cheaper to buy a bunker that is secure than to build a secure one. The Swiss government's price for the bunkers varies from several hundred thousand dollars to a couple of million. The government sells about twenty of the bunkers every year."

He turned and motioned for them to leave. "Now, for the video and some refreshments."

The coffee and strudel that were served as they watched the ten-minute video were great. Amy focused on the video and liked what she saw.

"I'm impressed," she said. "How long have you been open for deposits?"

"Only the last thirty years. In 1991, the Swiss government opened up some of the bunkers built during World War II. Our company bought the rights from the Swiss government and converted several to store bullion. Many others are just relics."

She answered the question he was too polite to ask: how much gold and silver bullion was the Prowers family looking to store?

"My family's bits and pieces of gold and silver are in several banks. We've decided to consolidate in one vault. We want secrecy and security, and you've showed us you have both. Many thanks for this impressive tour." She told him that she and her cousin were looking at the options for the family. "Please give us some time to decide."

Wilhelm smiled. "The size of our vaults buried in the mountain is not something we actively push. But Miss Prowers, no need to rush. When you decide, we will be here. We also have several other bunkers nearby that are just as secure."

He escorted the two of them to the car, and she thanked him again.

As they started down the mountain road back to Zurich, Amy said, "Bob, this bunker is too commercial for the Count. I can't see him running around the mountains and hiding his gold."

Bob agreed but asked, "Where would they take it when they arrived in Zurich?"

"Who knows? They're all dead, the Count and Marton's father. Frederic could be dead. But I know this, Bob; it has to be someplace simple and easy to get to. So now, it's back to Zurich," said Amy.

Just in time, she stopped herself from saying she wondered what Ace might have found in the records. They had said enough. No need to give Julian any information. She wasn't sure whose side he was on. Then, she laughed. What difference did it make today? If he was a plant for one of the right-wing groups, even Bazyli Czartoryski, then did it matter? No.

Her phone buzzed. It was Ace. All he had found in the accounting books were expenditures on the villas. She knew it was time to return to Berlin. Her search for the gold had been for Vince, his dream, but he died long before Frederic moved the gold to Switzerland. If Vince hadn't died, then maybe he would have found it. Maybe.

The search is over for me, she thought.

Regardless, it was hard for her to think that the Count hadn't told anyone or left information on the location of the storage vault and the security codes needed to get into the vault. Sonora was the logical one he would tell. But her aunt was adamant that she didn't know anything about the gold—except that it went to Switzerland.

"The search is over for me, Ace. We're at a dead end."

"Yeah, but you got to see some different parts of Germany, and I got to see Austria. And now Switzerland. Besides, we had no plan on what to do with the gold. Did we?"

"No, other than the obvious: to set up a charitable foundation. I never thought much about that. We certainly wouldn't keep it. At least so far, the right-wing groups haven't found it."

"Yes," said Ace. "Frankly, that's good enough for me. I'll book a flight back to Berlin for us." He laughed. "So, Amy, this means you're ready at long last to get involved with the Committee?"

"Yes, Ace, I'm ready. I hope I get excited about being part of the group."

"You will."

They both laughed, knowing working with Sonora was always interesting.

CHAPTER FORTY

Postscript

Berlin was consumed in a driving rainstorm. Unable to walk outside, Sonora found herself pacing from room to room in her mansion. Her mind kept going over what, if anything, no matter how trivial, her husband might have said about the gold. He had been dead more than five years, dying in Berlin two weeks after a trip to Zurich with Marton's father. She knew family and friends thought he would have told her how to access or find the gold. But he didn't. Or did he, and she had missed his clues?

She found herself in the study—really, *his* study. She recalled how, after his return from Switzerland, he had spent most of his time in this room reading. She stood in the center of the room. He was reading—but what? The walls were lined with books on almost every subject in the world. That was her husband, always reading.

Ah, I remember.

She walked over to a small chest sitting on a table. It was light-brown, almost blond, wood with gold inlays. It had a lock but no key, and she remembered that it had a false bottom. It came from the ancient caravansaries that crossed the Arabian Peninsula—at least, that was what the Count had told her when he brought it back from Yemen.

When he returned from Zurich, she had found him reading *The Southern Gates of Arabia*, written by Freya Stark in 1936. Freya had to be a strong woman to travel to that part of the world so many years ago. The Count said that she would like Freya, and he wanted her to read the book, which he had found in a bookshop in Yemen.

She opened the chest and saw the book, worn and thin, inside. He said that reading it made him feel like he was in Arabia without actually being there. From it, he had learned to understand the love and the hate that made up the Middle East. Why had he put it in the chest?

Sonora, you should read it every year, at least a chapter or two.

When he said that to her, she had laughed. But he repeated that to her several times after he came back from Zurich.

She opened the book, the old pages sticking together. Separating them, she found, to her surprise, a dedication the Count had written to her on the title page: "My dear, one day, you will find the treasure within this book." He had signed it: "Your loving husband."

For a moment, Sonora paused and allowed herself to remember the wonderful years they had together. She looked again at the title page. Below his signature were some figures. The numbers made no sense. They were not safe combinations, but having traveled the world, she thought they could be latitude and longitude.

Getting up, she looked at the rows of books in the library. She found one on maps of the world and pulled out Western Europe. After all, why would the Count be giving a location on another continent?

Turning the pages, she found a map of Europe and looked for latitude forty-seven degrees and longitude eight degrees. The coordinates put her in the center of Zurich. From conversations with Bob and Amy, she knew the Swiss government had a bullion storage vault in the city.

Yes, that makes sense.

Her husband would never have gone traipsing through the Alps with trucks loaded with gold. Too many eyes in the little villages, and he always got car sick.

For a moment, she wished she still smoked. Now was the time for a cigarette. Instead, she poured herself a small glass of brandy from the crystal bottle on the table. The gold was stored in the Swiss government vault in Zurich, which meant the access code was somewhere.

She picked up the book again and turned to the next page. To her amazement, in front of her was what everyone had been trying to find. In his handwriting was written: "Sonora, your name is the password," and beside it was a twenty-digit code. How like him to have used her name.

The brandy warmed her, and she poured more into her glass. So, the gold was in the Zurich bullion storage facility, guarded by the Swiss government. She knew intuitively that the book held the only copy of the vault's location and access codes. The Count never did duplicate; he had said it was his way of maintaining security.

What do I do with these codes? My husband left them to me, not to the world.

Putting the brandy glass down on the table, she looked at the codes again. Over the years, a billion dollars had been paid to relatives of Holocaust victims. It seemed that was as much justice as money could buy. Why resurrect the old and still-seething prejudices and hatred?

What purpose would be served finding the gold? I cannot think of one.

She shut the book and placed it in the false bottom of the chest. Perhaps one day, Amy would find it. Or perhaps not.

Epilogue

The cold grey days of a Berlin winter gave way to spring. Now the sun bathed the study in Sonora's home, and Amy found herself looking at the shelves filled with the Count's books. Many she had read, many not. She paused at the small wooden chest from Yemen and wondered if she would ever visit the country.

Opening the top of the chest, she was surprised to see a book inside. It was by Freya Stark, "The Southern Gates of Arabia". To read it would be like traveling with Freya in Yemen.

Closing the lid, she put the book in her sweater pocket. The smell of coffee permeated the room. She would get a cup and settle down to read Freya's travels.

Notes for the Reader

The Swiss in World War II

Switzerland benefited from being neutral in World War II by exchanging gold for Swiss francs, the only currency outside the US dollar that was accepted during the war. It made the Swiss an enabler of the Third Reich. Estimates were that over ninety percent of the German gold ended up in Swiss banks. Some of the German gold was from countries they conquered, like Austria, Belgium, the Netherlands, and Norway. Other gold was taken from private citizens or victims of concentration camps. When the war ended, the Swiss, afraid of adverse publicity and public opinion, agreed to pay over two hundred fifty million. They claimed to have looked for heirs of unclaimed accounts.

In the Holocaust era, 1933 to 1945, over 6.8 million Swiss bank accounts were opened. When the committees from the United States and Switzerland began in 1999 to investigate bank accounts, over 2.7 million accounts had been destroyed, yet today, there are over 4.1 million Holocaust-era accounts in Swiss banks. More importantly, Swiss banks failed after the war to locate heirs of unclaimed accounts.

Gold Bullion Storage Vaults/Bunkers

Storing gold or silver in a vault is easier than opening a bank account. Minimum charges annually for a bullion vault can be less than a hundred dollars a year. There is no limit on how little or much bullion could be put in the vault. To open a bank account could take a half million dollars and servicing it could cost another couple thousand a year. The Swiss government tries to keep undesirables, the criminal element, from acquiring vaults/bunkers, but some criminal organizations do get in.

Discrimination Against Jews

Swiss banks had other bullion accounts, many for families that were in concentration camps. Wealthy Jews saw what was coming and set up the accounts to protect their assets. Everyone skips over how the money got into those accounts.

The Swiss government in 1938 made a decision to allow Germany to mark the passports of Jews with a 'J' stamp and in 1942 Switzerland sealed the borders to prevent racially persecuted persons with the stamp from entering. While many refugees were granted asylum, a more lenient policy could have saved thousands of refugees from being killed.

The Occult

In general, all Nazis believed in the occult. Astrology and the supernatural were part of the Third Reich. The top Nazis leaders used astrologers to assist in military planning. What was not so well known was that as Germany started to lose the war, the dire predictions of astrologers made those astrologers redundant.

The Nazis used occultism and the Eastern religions to explain to the German people a world that had gone against Germany. The supernatural drew them to the Nazis, and it was used by the Nazis.

Where is the Gold?

Finding the gold is difficult. It can be sitting in a vault/bunker requiring no service. Security is an issue as the vaults require identification.

The Hunt for Raubgold Discussion Questions

1. Would you have followed your dead husband's search after twenty years?
2. Do you think Frederic is alive?
3. Why is the Abbot playing both sides, Bazyli and Sonora?
4. What do you think happened to the gold?
5. Who is your favorite character?
6. Were you surprised the Vatican was involved?
7. Do you think Amy should continue the search—or will in the future?
8. Do you think the gold still exists, and will anyone eventually find it?
9. Do you think Amy's husband would have been disappointed that she gave up the search?

ABOUT THE AUTHOR
Katherine Burlake

Katherine qualified as one of the first women Air Force Officers to attend the Air Force Navy Intelligence School and serve in the Vietnam War.

Living in Thailand, England, and Germany led her to the Department of State and Broadcasting Board of Governors, reporting on embassy operations globally. She has traveled to over 130 countries, including Afghanistan and Iraq.

Katherine has been published in the *Macguffin*, The Face of War: A Baghdad Woman. Her vast experiences, plus her four years in Riyadh, Saudi Arabia working in the embassy, bring richness and depth to her engaging novels.

Colorado is now her home.

Discover **The Bystander**, the first book in the Amy Prowers mystery thriller series.

Saudi Arabia is the Perfect Sandstorm

The kingdom is at a crossroads with the leadership in the royal family, and it is in danger of losing its one-hundred-year-old, special relationship with the USA. Understanding a country that has stood behind a veil for the past century is difficult. In *The Bystander*, Saudi politics, culture, and the relationships of the royal family show how a Bedouin culture runs a country that is so vital to the world's oil supply. In Burlake's words, "Walk in the culture of Saudi Arabia, experience the desert, and understand how it has been formed by its history."

The Saudi king is dying, and a successor will be chosen from the grandsons of Abdul Aziz, the kingdom's founder. One royal prince, Rashid Abdul Aziz, is determined to rule, but royal blood is not enough. He needs to demonstrate he is worthy of the crown. If his wife can find the first Qur'an, used by the Prophet, then Prince Rashid will be the next king. Rashid needs someone he can trust. He asks Amy Prowers, the widow of an old friend, to assist his wife, Princess Hassa, on the excavation and validate the findings. Amy is eager to help but discovers there is more at stake than ancient cultures. The kingdom is a breeding ground for a new generation of terrorists. A secret terrorist sect called the Black Princes puts Amy's life at risk as she becomes a participant in her friend's quest for the Saudi throne.

The Last Request by Katherine Burlake—An Amazon best seller

Be careful who you trust …

The Last Request follows Amy Prowers as she reels from the untimely and suspicious death of her father in a plane crash. Explore in great depth as a daughter tries to find the truth behind the Shroud of Turin in a nation-hopping thriller guaranteed to satisfy fans of mystery and suspense.

She finds herself trying to fulfill his last request to her and is left with words of warning: ***Be careful who you trust***. Reluctantly, Amy leaves behind the family oil and gas business to enter into the world where both her parents lived in World War II. Now, she sees their past as her future.

Her journey takes her from the Balkans to Mexico as she tries to locate the real Shroud of Turin. A North African leader and former Nazis are also looking for the Shroud of Turin, and it becomes clear this journey will change Amy's life.